Seven Moves to Sahara Time

By Chris Nall-Evans

On a beach in Messina, Italy a child builds a sandcastle. It survives until the incoming tide and the local winds take it back to its rightful place. And the same thing will happen the following day. Everyday.

In a restaurant in Brighton, England a person orders a cafetiere of coffee. The waiter brings it along with a sand timer. The sand runs through to its base. The coffee is ready. And the same thing will happen the following day. Everyday.

The King watches every grain of sand that moves and becomes of something- of time, of physical embodiment, of status and watches it return to its natural state. He is pleased. He's particularly impressed at how long the pyramids have withstood time. He has been doing this for around 4.5 billion years. Now that's a job with staying power.

CONTENTS

CHAPTER 1

RUMBLINGS

Naples, Italy January 24 2020

Bishop Emilio sipped from his glass of lemon tea as he casually glanced over a few parish news papers. His mobile phone rang. He rummaged in his breast pocket and acknowledged the call. 'Holy father it is me Padre Alfonso. I'm hearing the voice again'. Bishop Emilio drew a deep sigh. This was to be the third phone call he had taken from Alfonso in the last 2 months. He breathed a little deeper than normal before he responded.

'Alfonso, why are you in so much spiritual pain? You have your little church, you are a man of considerable learning and love of the father, son and holy ghost. You have a good congregation, albeit a diminishing one, but we are all suffering with that. Pah, the temptations of the scientific method. What is the voice saying?'

'I'm confused father. I cannot rid myself of the vision of our lord and the lines from Isaiah. I hear them repeat:

> *Then they will go forth and look on the corpses of men who have transgressed against me. For their worm will not die and their fire will not be quenched and they will be an abhorrence to all mankind.*

I have this overwhelming sense of foreboding. It pains me greatly. Why should I worry about our lords return, as it surely will be? Man is everywhere fallen. Look at what is happening in Hubei province.'

Father Emilio shrugged to himself, took another sip and spoke.

'Alfonso my son, you are a good person. Be at peace with the now. Do not worry about tomorrow. I will see you shortly at our regular meeting'.

The JESTER interjects.....

A troubled man it would seem. Beset with his own pains and suffering. Surely a tortured soul? Who knows?

Oh, please forgive me for not introducing myself. I am your intermediary, your facilitator, your road map so to speak. A guide through the various pathways you are about to journey. Call me The JESTER. Truth be told, you could probably get through this without me but allow me to indulge a little personal ego and say that it's probably easier if I do.

However I'll try not to interfere too much along the way. After all said and done this is your journey, your imagination and I'm not tempted to exploit or manipulate that in any sense of the word. I'll catch you later.

Padre Alfonso put down the the phone. He filled a kettle and put it on his 2 ring burner. An instant coffee with a sprinkle of whitener. Every morning at 11 a.m. Another ritual observed. He stirred in the white powder and sat down, contemplating the weekend sermon. Below his flat on the San Sebastiono, a busy road feeding the centre of Naples, next to the holy church of Santa Maria Della Mercede, motor cars, scooters and bicycles hooted, screeched and made other noises as if to attract attention. He hears nothing.

'This weekend I will make my sermon centre around the language of sacrifice' he mutters to himself.

He leafs through his battered copy of the testaments unable to find a suitable passage from which to make a start. He goes to the window and stares out. He turns and faces the crucifix hanging on the wall opposite. 'Sacrifice.....'

....

Bristol. UK. November 2019

The whiff of cigarette smoke, sweat and unwashed clothes lingered in Phil's flat. It's Thursday afternoon and Phil hadn't left his home for 3 days, having binged on a box set of some war games that his sister bought him for his last birthday. Age 24.

There are empty crisp and cake packets strewn over his coffee table and unfinished bottles of coke, lager and water. This is what Phil would call his workstation. Cigarette butts anywhere but in the tray. Phil is sitting on a moth eaten chair still wearing the baggy pyjamas he put on 2 weeks ago. They've seen better days as well.

His laptop stares at him from a nearby make do desk alongside a main frame computer and an HP tablet. He turns his attention to a page he has open on his laptop. It's his blogger page. On the screen of his mainframe computer he has rolling news items which traverse the page at a little better than snail pace. At this precise moment the news centres on several protests and varieties of direct action against the erection of 5G masts in various parts of the UK and mainland Europe.

'Shit, it's really happening' Phil observed. On his blog page he started to write some (throwaway) comments about 5G masts, radioactive emissions and discharges which, he contributes, are the primary cause of many of the world's so called natural disasters and public health emergencies.

He lit an H&B and casually took a draw. The world of Phil is a conspiracy wet dream. If it isn't a conspiracy, it's not worth the effort.

His upbringing didn't help. Raised by his father after his mum had died in 2005 following a sudden and unexplained illness, he didn't find it easy to fend for himself. His father crashed into a long episode of depression shortly after her passing and following the common process of denial, self blame and guilt, both father and son in their own ways started to search for other answers. His elder sister got knocked up at 19, left home and that was that. Phil was left to get on with things. Not an easy or indeed enjoyable boyhood experience. He left home at 17; his father would make sure he had enough to live on, albeit meagre, but the Armed Forces did at least look after their own and as Phil's father had seen active duty in Kosovo, Iraq and Afghanistan, by the time of his enforced retirement he had accrued a decent pension. So Phil was generally comfortable. But as for mum: find someone to blame.

Phil sat down and sent a message. It's to his friend and another conspiracy nerd, Rick. 'Hey, come on over tonight. Finished the war games. Easy. Beat my previous score. Let's put some more stuff on the Conspire to Convince blog. I think we should have a few bevvies on the reaction to our earlier blog. Mate, they're reacting. Big style. OMG. And bring some eats, pls…'

....

Seville, Spain August 2019

'Hey Gabriella, you finished in the shower yet?' Yelled Jose. It was a hot August day in the Bellavista-La Palmera district of Seville, home to Real Betis football club. Juan got no response for a while and when Gabriella finally emerged, scrunching her hair with a towel, he kicked off. 'How many times a day do you need to shower, woman. Jeez I know it's hot but I needed to have a dump.'

Gabriella walked back to the bedroom without answering and muttered some comments under her breath.

It had been a tough couple of months leading up to August. Gabriella had just come out of a long term relationship with a personal trainer and it had ended after she had found out he was cheating on her. She had screamed and shouted, threatened violence, destroyed most of his belongings and walked out of his life. Then there was the social media character assassination. Photographs, accusations, threats and it took a local magistrates court order against her to eventually calm things down.

She had found Jose, in all truth, on the rebound. He was pleasant enough and seemed to care for her in a different way to the personal trainer. She liked his sense of commitment. A good catholic boy from a fairly decent family. He would do, for now.

Gabriella spent her working days in a local travel agency near the centre of Seville, about a half hour ride from her home. It paid her a wage and she enjoyed helping out clients searching for their holiday of a lifetime.

But her passion was modelling. Gabriella was quite a stunner. She had 'good form' as her agent would say. She had enough income to hire an agent who promised her the world in all it's glitter and celebrity. But apart from coming 3rd in a local talent contest and an audition to advertise a cleaning fabric she had got nowhere. Despite all this, she persisted. Her friend Anna had suggested she try for the big stuff like Spain's Got Talent or Love Island but she didn't feel the call. 'Fuck Anna, trying to put me out there in the spotlight, only to like, get splattered. I know her.' But for all her criticism she still went out with her and got drunk together.

Jose had switched on the TV and Gabriella joined him on the sofa. She cuddled up to him, gave him a squeeze and made a grab for his crotch. 'Cheer up man' she cried, and picked up a copy of Spanish Vogue. Three minutes into the mag pictures and Gabriella was already making nasty comments about some of the models….. 'look at her lips….. look at her ass…… look at the lashes on her…..' it went on. Jose had learned to switch off from the bitchiness.

He picked up a travel brochure that Gabriella had brought home and turned to South America. They had talked of taking a vacation together. Peru, Ecuador, Chile? Holiday, adventure, retreat? And then a thought came at him from the right side.

She never says Gracias.

………………………………………………….

Stuttgart 2017

Katrin had signed off the compliance papers that verified the structural integrity of the office block complex in Agadir. The whole project had been complicated, not least because the city of Agadir, on Morocco's southern coast had been devastated by earthquake in 1960 and safety was not only a priority. It was an obsession. And then there was the inevitable local politics to circumvent and, she supposed, the slipping of a few hundred thousand euros in a few people's pockets. But she didn't want to know about that. Her job as a senior architect required everything within her control to be absolutely watertight; what the politicians did was up to them. She didn't have much time for politicians, referring to them as amateurs with no direction and certainly no qualification.

According to the project management brief, the building would be competed by Autumn 2018.

She returned home from her city offices in Stuttgart. A busy day and a relaxing evening to look forward to. Her partner Sven had promised a candle lit meal with a bottle of Piesporter to celebrate the completion of the contract papers and the news that Sven had landed a plumb job with an international aid agency. True to form, the table was laid out and the candles lit. Van Morrison, one of Katrin's favourite "old school" singers, was playing on the Sonos.

Sven had chosen to keep the surprise job a little secret for them to toast after the main course. It was all about finding the right time to broach the subject. Sven wasn't sure how Katrin would take this, because the terms and conditions required Sven to spend considerable amounts of time away, usually in war torn or distressed regions of the world.

Katrin broke that bit of silence first. 'So, you said on the phone that you'd had some information from Medicin Sans Frontieres, let's hear it then'. Sven read out the letter he'd received that morning. Katrin whooped and raised her glass. 'Wunderbar, wunderbar' she cheered as she clunked her glass with Sven's. 'When do you start?'
He skipped around the awkward bits of the contract for the time it took to finish off a second bottle of Piesporter and then presented the bit about travel away to her. To his surprise Katrin seemed non plussed about it, maybe she was too drunk to appreciate the issue, maybe she was suppressing her alarm, maybe she actually was OK about it all. They talked further until Katrin started to nod and Sven took the hint, switched off the lights and escorted her to bed.

January 2019

The project in Agadir had completed 5 months late and way over budget. Katrin had been asked by her boss to travel over and check up on the final build. She booked a GermanWings flight from Stuttgart to Marrakesh. Sven was working in Myanmar on a community renovation project and had sent many messages to her and his office bosses about the disturbing hostilities between Muslim and Buddhist factions in the region.

Her flight was on time and as the Boeing 737 took off she plugged in her earphones to listen to some Bob Dylan and later, for a lighter mood, Fleetwood Mac. 'Don't Stop Thinking About Tomorrow' was playing out as the aircraft landed. This would be her first visit to Morocco, indeed to an Arab country.

She had read about the 1970's, how Morocco was part of the hippie experience, about Hideous Kinky and of course the famous single by Crosby Stills and Nash. She hummed the tune as she walked through passport control '.......don't you know we're riding on the Marrakesh Express....'

From Marrakesh she took a taxi to Agadir, a 3 hour uneventful ride, which straddled late morning and post lunch, and apart from seeing a few goats perched dangerously in the trees alongside the road the trip was one to forget. One for the tourists, she guessed.

Her contact met her at the office complex and talked her through the guide. They took a quick bite and the lead contract manager took them around the complex. Everything seemed in order. Nevertheless Katrin wasn't impressed with the way the locals conducted themselves over the course of the afternoon. Her Aryan sense of superiority kicked in; she couldn't help it. A double first in Architecture at the University of Heidelberg followed by a Masters degree in Applied Mathematics certainly gives one elevation. Under her breath she just muttered and made a few notes.

Katrin waited for the contract taxi to arrive and take her back to Marrakesh. Tonight she would stay at a Riad in the tourist area. She arrived in Marrakesh after 8, took a quick shower and strolled out to the restaurant nearby, the one she picked out on Trip Advisor. The recommendation was 3 meat Tagine which she took and finished off with a plate of dates and nuts. In the background Leonard Cohen's 'So Long Marianne' was playing. 'Cool place' she thought.

She walked back to her Riad, and took in the vibrant colours of the interior. Before her head hit the pillow she had wished she had made this journey in the 1970's. Back to the concrete jungle tomorrow.

………………………………………………..

Bogota, Colombia. Autumn 2019.

It had try to heal itself after the drug barons had been caught and locked up. A social contract with the criminal classes to try and restore some face and dignity in Colombia's capital.

And it had worked to a large extent. The criminals had been paid off for keeping the peace after the arrest and incarceration of one of Colombia's top drug barons. The government and the paramilitary group the FARC had worked a truce. And the politicians seemed to have learned the lesson that you can't live on the proceeds of cocaine alone. You need tourists, you need trust. Bogota, so the tourist board said, is so safe even the Pope came here (in 2017).

The tourist board failed to mention Pablo Mendes. City councillor. Bogota city council had 45 councillors and was the highest political and second highest administrative authority in Colombia. Responsible for all the city's administration, the city councillors were elected by popular vote for a 4 yr term, and subject to re-election. Pablo Mendes had survived 5 terms of office. Although never making the much desired office of principal mayor, he had a place on the council as deputy leader of the centre right group and had also been chief whip. He had survived a near assassination attempt back in 2015 when a revolutionary protest group had staged several para military attempts at bringing down the council. Now he travelled with 2 or 3 "buddies", heavies who knew how to take people down where necessary and leave little evidence.

Mendes lived a grandiose lifestyle, much more than his public service salary would command and was able to avoid or deflect questions about the source of his lavish tastes. The press chose, or were pressured to choose, to avoid embarrassing questions. Married with 3 children, Mendes always visited church on a Sunday morning, would drop off his family and would then visit the brothels he ran, through an intermediary, in the afternoon. He couldn't resist some free 'placer sexual', and while he was to the girls, La Boss, he enjoyed the sexual fruits of his criminal activity most weekends. The visit to the brothels also gave him an opportunity to check on his drugs investment. Nothing as big as the previous drug barons had - that would have come to the attention of the authorities too easily. No, just a sideline to keep the hookers under control and a few lackies to do his dirty washing. And he always covered his back.

The city hall had been cleaned up, hence the boast by the tourist board about Bogota being a safe place to visit. But in the back streets and the slums, far away from the Plaza de Bolivar and the historic buildings crime paid.

But things were getting tough. Bit by bit the city hall was fulfilling its pledge to clean up the city 'root and branch.' Mendes had managed to pay off a few low life crooks but he knew he couldn't buck the trend for much longer. The newspapers were no longer prepared to be bought off and the TV companies had been given a decent amount of broadcasting freedom. It was only a matter of time before he would be exposed. So Mendes had started to look at doing business beyond the confines of his native home country, but truth be told, he didn't have his heart in it.

Renata Mendes knew what Pablo was up to, to a point. She knew he played around with the dirt of the city and wasn't naive to the fact that they had many things people of a similar status were denied. She kept it to herself. Pablo wasn't the kind of man you argued with. He came from a long line of macho persuasion that claimed a wife as ownership of a commodity. She had been on the receiving end of his fist and learned to keep things under wraps or suffer the consequences. She hated the bastard. But, for the sake of the children she put up. He had threatened to leave her several times during their 32 years of marriage, but, she guessed, they were empty threats designed to maximise compliance. After all, in a catholic country like Colombia if you were to lose your husband you lost your dignity, your livelihood, and, if you had one, your future.

So Renata kept up the pretence of being a loving wife. She had patience but she knew her time would come.

……………………………………………………………..

Lyons, France. November 2019.

Pierre stumbled back into the restaurant kitchen via the swing doors. 'Customer on table 17, said take it back, it's overcooked, and furthermore it's got far too much wine in the ragu, sorry chef. Can you knock up another steak? Sorry chef.' Alain looked at the clock hovering over the large microwave and shouted under his breath, 'Jeez, it's 8.54pm, doesn't anyone get a break in this restaurant?'

The kitchen always closed at 9pm, weekdays and weekends. The money stopped at 9pm even though all the staff were expected to clean up the debris in advance for the following day. Nobody left before 9.30, but that wasn't going to happen tonight. A fresh steak and another attempt at keeping the spoilt, self serving, unsympathetic clients happy in order to keep the Michelin rating.

Chef tonight happened to be Alain Didier. Head chef. Usually he made a point of being around to keep the kitchen staff in check, supervise the food preparation and sometimes prepare a sauce or a soup but rarely would Alain be late out of 'Le Arts Nouveau', a fine dining restaurant in the posh suburbs of Lyons. Tonight however was different as two of the staff were off, apparently ill, and so he had to step up. Alain was a hot chef, trained at the Institut de Gourmet, Rue la Bourse and took the accolade, personally for getting the restaurant its Michelin stars and keeping them for the 3rd year running.

Alain had a love/hate approach to his work. Well it was probably more a hate/hate approach. He liked the bossing around and the eternal looking for faults in people, side of the job. He saw this as his calling, the only way to ensure perfection, bollock everyone. He had gone off the grafting side of the job and felt that actual cooking was now beneath his station in life. In his own words, to himself mostly, he'd say "I've moved on". Most of the staff despised him, intensely. The topic of a post shift spliff induced random conversation was usually about Alain and his temper, Alain and his overeating, Alain and his smelly pet dog etc etc.

9.50 pm. Lights off in the kitchen. Alain declined to sit at the bar and unwind with a drink. He picked up his coat from the rail near the bar and looked around towards table 17 but whoever it was that dared to challenge his cooking had left. Only a few punters were left in the place now and most were on coffee and liqueurs. He said his good-nights to the owner, waited 15 minutes before he took a tram from nearby the restaurant and travelled the 9 stops to his flat in the banking district of Lyons. His flat was on the 7th floor and he impatiently unlocked the outer door. His mail box was empty and he discovered that the lift was out of order, yet again. He climbed the 7 floors and nearly collapsed as he opened his front door. He fell into the hall and was met with a lick to his ear by his 3 year old cocker spaniel.

Alain went into the kitchen, which certainly would not command a wooden star never mind a Michelin star, and took out a Hawaiian pizza from the fridge, put on the oven and dispassionately placed the pizza in the centre. A 12 minute meal for one. The dog got fed, eventually, and after both had full bellies, Alain decided that a late walk was probably a walk too much, especially given the state of the lift and hoped that doggie would not shit in the lounge tonight. Alain relied on his neighbour to give it some exercise when he was out and had entrusted the flat key to her. The neighbour, a middle aged widow, enjoyed the opportunity to get out of the flat and take a walk in the local park, proudly walking with the mut at her side. To anyone who asked she would say that the dog was hers. Of course she never divulged any of this to Alain. That would be far too risky.

…………………………………………………

Boston. USA. December 2019.

'So, in terms of milestones for the next quarter I'd like to see you achieve a further 5-6 clients to add to your area of work. I think you could improve on your work performance and we're really looking at strong, positive client feedback which seems to have escaped you over the past half of the year. Let's not yet call this a wake up call but I gotta say we'll be watching how you perform. We're in this business to make money, and my job is to earn and add value to this company. If you fail then I fail and I don't like failure. That'll be all Graham.'

Mitch had just conducted another employee appraisal. Ruthless, as ever. He demanded more than any other line manager in the Cyclops corporation. And co workers knew it. Quarterly appraisal was nothing to look forward to if you worked under Mitch Ginsberg.

The Cyclops Corporation was becoming a major player in the well developed silicon chip market and intelligence systems. Trading had been very good despite less than perfect stock market conditions and the company had earned a reputation for hard talk but fair play. Mitch Ginsberg had been there from the beginning. He had worked with the current CEO many years ago to develop some imaginative and highly lucrative IT solutions. Starting off in a lock up over 23 years ago, both Mitch and Desi Sowami , the head of Cyclops, had brought together their ideas, invested their money and took a risk at pitching the business to the American economy.

That was 23 years ago. Now Desi was CEO and Mitch still a line manager, albeit quite a senior one. Mitch was getting frustrated, though he contained it most of the time. His hunger for power was partly tempered by his deal with the company over his salary. He had managed to negotiate a sales commission to augment his salary. So he was pretty well off as long as the company was doing well. Hence the hard line appraisals. But the money wasn't enough. There was absolutely no opportunity at present to climb the greasy pole, and Desi was going nowhere.

The company recognised that Mitch brought in good revenue to the business. Mitch knew it too. He had great contacts and was a brilliant net-worker. And boy could he negotiate. Most people in the company couldn't quite work out why he hadn't ascended to deputy CEO or at least senior commercial manager.

Mitch had worked it out. He would do things very differently if he had the reins of power. Perhaps Desi had got wind of this and didn't like a regime change. Maybe Desi thought he was a threat. Who knows. But Mitch worked out his strategy like a master-class chess player. He would slowly destroy his superiors. Given his access to confidential files and company archives he could see a way to fulfil his ambition.

He had been raised in a household where perfection was the standard. You had to major at sport, school and in respect to your elders. 'You gotta measure up and make me proud' was the maternal command. His father was no less demanding, often saying 'I'm doing this for your own damn good' as he then went on to publicly admonish him.

So Mitch worked to get his parental approval. It wasn't easy. But, he supposed there was one consolation. No other siblings, no-one else to compete with for fatherly attention and applause. He'd seen this sort of thing go on among some of his high school friends. Always competing with the elder sister, or younger brother for mummy's smile.

On his sixteenth birthday he was given a watch, a very prestigious watch, which had been handed down from the family over several generations. 'Take good care of this, son' said his father. 'It's never lost a minute. Never. That's going to be you. That's what you must be like, my great grand-daddy's watch.'

From that point on Mitch would check his watch, on the hour, every hour. It never failed to keep time.

CHAPTER 2

MOVEMENT

The JESTER speaks

So there you have it…. the magnificent seven? The seven deadly sins? The seven seas of Rhye! It'll be for you to decide. Pythagoras, he of the wise Greeks of old thought the number seven to be the perfect number; the addition of three plus four; the triangle and the square.

Then of course, the seven wonders of the world, well the human world anyway. And didn't apostle John in the book of Revelation obsess over the number? Seven churches, and perhaps to go to that darker side the number of heads of the three beasts 7x7x7. And of course the number is prime. The lucky seven, Oh, I could go on.

As I said earlier, I'm just the go between, a guide to navigate between this world and the world of the other. Oh, yes my friend. The place inhabited by these people is not the only world. In another place, perhaps even another dimension, other events are in play. Significant events indeed. Little do these people know about what will eventually confront them. And when I introduce you to it, as I must, I am duty bound to take on a different persona. But that is yet to come.

For now let's see how life for the seven mortals proceeds…………

Protests against 5G technology continued in to the 2019 Christmas season in many countries in Europe. A well organised group of conspiracy theorists had embarked on a campaign of arson, social media misinformation and collective action in parts of mainland Britain. Protesters were claiming that the technology emitted harmful radiation to those living near the masts.

Phil was circulating on the social media blog that the threat was very real, making claims that he was one of the first to establish this health connection. He watched the tweets and the responses increase in their thousands. "Man this is amazing" he shouted back at his mate....all the while not sure whether he believed what he wrote and certainly unable to verify any of the claims to anything remotely scientific. "Bill Gates is the anti Christ" people were tweeting.

Whilst this media attention did wonders for Phil's ego, he was less than happy with any attempts to get him to appear or meet up with anyone else who was in the same mindset. Phil had turned down dozens of , probably inconsequential, offers to meet up to say this or write that. He did however agree to write an article for the anarchist magazine Conspire to Convince magazine, for which he received the princely sum of £200. Amongst a readership of around 11,000 on the dark web, Phil saw this as his finest hour (well, about 50 minutes worth of typing to be correct).

As preparations for Christmas were being undertaken in Europe, the news started to drip feed of an outbreak of a new virus in Wuhan, China. At an early stage of infection, most of Europe wasn't bothered or interested, the UK was still battling a general election with Brexit being fought as the main, if only agenda item. It was China's problem. Europe was more interested in whether the UK was to be the first country to leave the 28 member state of the EU. Britain was more concerned about getting goods across the English channel.

By December, Wuhan had recorded a number of admissions to hospital but no fatalities.... the new year would bring with it news of the worst kind as the virus spread its ugly tentacles beyond China to mainland Europe. On the 26 December there was a magnitude 5 earthquake near the epicentre of the outbreak in Wuhan. No fatalities.

But Phil made it clear in his blog that the earthquake had cracked part of the substructure of the laboratory where the outbreak came from. Maybe it did, maybe it didn't. "That should shake up the world" he smiled, smugly.

………………………..

Snow was falling in Boston as busy shoppers were out buying essentials and presents for the holiday season. Tweet Tweet, the city's busy toy store was full with a small crowd gathering outside. Taxi cabs were being hailed and the coffee shops filled with festive and other gossip.

This sort of behaviour didn't resonate much with Mitch. He and his wife had both made the decision not to have children so the bringing up toddler and junior part of life never touched them. Neither did they play the uncle and aunt role much as Rachel, his wife didn't get on with her younger brother and family and anyway, they lived down state. It would be another quiet Christmas.

Back at the Cyclops HQ, Mitch was about to chair a disciplinary hearing. He would make it a quick event. On his own. Final warning. Mitch called in the co-worker and got him seated. In the background 'The Ride of the Valkyries' played. Mitch always played this if there was a disciplinary. It boosted his energy no end and was immediately off putting to the stranger in the room, a classic zero-sum game that Mitch would play. For an appraisal he might choose 'O Fortuna', another shrill piece of classical music. How he got away with it nobody knew, but when he was in the chair no-one challenged him. 6 minutes into the hearing and the employee walked out, tail between leg, with a final warning.

Mitch looked up in his diary and picked up the telephone. 'Karen, get me the commercial manager for Ingosec, his number is in the book.'

Ingosec was one of Cyclops customers and had purchased over $30,000 of customised IT infrastructure around 6 months ago. It worked a lot with the far east market, especially Hong Kong and Taiwan. It had paid off around a third of the amount but found that work was drying up as the impact of the virus in the far east started to kick in.

Mitch would have to deal with it. Desi, the CEO had asked him to intervene personally after Oscar, a fellow co-worker and senior to Mitch had apparently overlooked the payment dates and thereby failed to contact them. Unbeknown to Desi, Mitch had deliberately failed to inform Oscar about the build up of debt that was happening with the intention of getting Oscar a bad reputation as a person who took his eye off the ball: the long game was to get Oscar's job. Then to the top.

Mitch spoke gruffly down the phone. In a nutshell it was pay up or we'll see you in court. Despite protestations by the boss about the state of Ingosec's current balance sheet and trading conditions all Mitch would say is 'China is not my problem, you are my problem. $20,000 plus interest is my problem. Fix it or be sued.'

No Christmas cheer for Ingosec Inc. And a new year resolution: treat Oscar as your lap dog. Mitch was a happy man. Quick watch check.

…………………………………………………………

Jose had completed his Christmas shop. He had chosen a teddy bear coat for Gabriella. Not a cheap buy, but not outrageous either. He wasn't sure how long this relationship would last so he had decided not to over commit. Gabriella, on the other hand had bought Jose a ring. Well, maybe it's a bit early, she thought, but she felt she could trust him and he was as close to her as anyone she had previously dated. Each of them had kept their Christmas shopping a secret. In Seville the Christmas season was in full swing with the church bells ringing out and plans afoot for a month of festive services.

Gabriella was noticeably excited when she caught up with her friend Anna in a local coffee shop along the Guadalqivir river front.

'Hey Anna, guess what. I like got a model shoot next month at the Foxy Studios.' Anna seemed less than impressed, but Gabriella failed to notice. 'It's modelling for cosmetic dentistry, Face upwards, no tits and ass!'

'Coolio, Gabbs you have the face for it and the mouth' replied Anna, in a slightly disparaging tone. Again Gabriella failed to read the signals. 'You told Jose yet?' asked Anna. Gabriella said that she had not as she had only received the email this very morning, but that she would when he was next over.

'But, Anna, here's like the main thing. This guy who contacted me reckons he can get me some proper modelling work, maybe even some minor parts in a movie that he's making. He wants me to go to Madrid to his modelling studio to see if I make the grade and have the right figure and voice. This could be a whole new career.' Gabriella reached into her fake Prada handbag and dived into her edition of the Spanish glossy magazine '@Ola' and flicked through the pictures.

Anna sunk her mouth into her chai latte. She could see where this was going.

………………………………………..

Restaurant bookings at Les Arts Nouveau were at a high throughout December. Party crowds from Lyons and its environs, office celebrations and the occasional retirement. The owners had a lot to be optimistic about. Rave reviews, faithful returners and a cool atmosphere meant that the restaurant had it all. And of course it boasted its Michelin star status and chef. But Alain wasn't happy. He'd had enough of the pressure to please. And he wanted a change. No going back to chasing star ratings and excellence again, time to get out of the kitchen. He had the thought of possibly going into further education at the nearby Vittel polytechnic in their excellent catering and hotel management suite. With his reputation he was confident he'd have a pretty good chance at obtaining work and from there build up a new career. He had heard that they were hiring for the new year, so went on-line and found a vacancy, part time, in the hospitality department. Opportunity knocks.

He downloaded the application form and gathered together his CV. Now a bit tired and in need of updating, his credentials were sufficient enough, in his mind to at least get a chance at interview. Just tidy up the last couple of years, spin a bit of this and that and then walk the dog.

…………………………………………………….

Christmas came and went in the house of Katrin and Sven. It had been a typical German occasion, with enough of a snowfall to call it Christmas weather and they had met up with some old friends and visited family in Munich over the new year period. They both made resolutions to travel together more in 2020 and to try and get a better life/work balance.

Sven had been in post for over 9 months now and had travelled to an assortment of far flung countries helping out with the fallout from earthquake, famine, flood and other disasters. It had made him much more humble, emapthetic and glad to be in the company of his partner, Katrin, whenever he could find time to fly home. Katrin had obtained a promotion within the engineering company she worked for and had worked on a number of high profile building designs after the one she had signed off in Agadir. She was hungry for a break and some sun. Work had consumed her over the past year and the call of Morocco was loud in her head. Both Katrin and Sven headed off to the gym for their daily work out and then finished off the morning with a deli take away. The snow was falling again and a light blanket of the white stuff had settled on the cars in the street.

When they got home Katrin opened a bottle of Merlot and poured out 2 drinks. 'Let's go to Morocco' she said, out of nowhere. 'What, now?' replied Sven, jokingly. 'Duhh, no, dummie, let's agree to go to Morocco the earliest we can both get away. I'm missing the chaos, the colour and heat of Marrakesh. I need a break. It's OK for you my love, seeing all these exotic places as part of your work, but I'm rooted in an office in Stuttgart and I'm overdue for some leave. I can ask for some time off between now and end April.'

Sven responded by saying that he couldn't say when he would be able to get any meaningful time off his work. 'Famine doesn't follow office hours', he sighed.

CHAPTER 3

ANOTHER PLACE

Stillness dominates the space that was once a towering castle. A form like no other form seen on mortal earth. To say 'a towering castle' is not entirely accurate, but it helps to signify that the place is suffused with a sense of regal pomp, but should not be confused with a castle or palace in the literal sense, for indeed, in this void of space and time sits an old man, again a form immediately understandable to the mortal world but not a man in the true sense.. it is a being with absolute control.

The space that he resides in has no colour and little form. It was once a regal palace and the colours were so intense that any being in there would have to avert their gaze or be blinded. It was a majestic space, from the time that mighty explosion took place and colour, matter and indeed everything else came to life. But the colour has slowly faded and matches the sadness in the heart of the old King and everything he owns seems to be slipping away and advancing, but at the same time shrinking. He thinks in the colour black.

The JESTER is walking with ease upon tumble-down ruins of sandstone walls and pillars. A wisp not bound to life and death. The old man, a King in all that he beholds cannot see or hear him. Next to this king hangs a skeleton, well that again is a play on words, imagine if you will a torso, so lean and skinny it may as well be a skeleton. It is barely possible to distinguish the torso from the grey and muddy walls that it hangs on.

The JESTER speaks.

Me again. Different place different dimension now my friends. You may be a little confused. Remember what I said? I'm here to guide you as you pass through this pageant. But I must also intercede with the powers that be in the sands of time.

And I'll have to change my tone somewhat, that becoming of a jester in the royal court. Etiquette I believe it is called. Wait. No. Heavens! Can you see? Others! You! - Wait - come back! Please, come back! Please don't leave me! Stay around, you won't be disappointed.

'Now, to matters of importance. Location. Ahh, the Saharan desert - place of mysteries and ancient secrets. Lost cities and civilizations. People speaking in strange tongues.

Thousands of miles of nothing but sand and desolation. But only the uninitiated eye would walk past its endless treasures and stories, as kingdoms and legends roamed these plains before our time. But we are inside this region, we are of this region, we ARE this region.

Some say that the desert was made by the gods for man to find its place in the world. To accept the faith that is bestowed on all of us. To find a way to cheat death. Hahahaha.

But let's not start with the dark themes here, shall we? What about faith?

As all men of faith walked the sands of eternity. As did Christ to withstand the temptation of the devil, as did Moses to free his people, as did the Mohammed prophet on the day of his birth. Inshala. But as they lived for our souls only the traveller by himself can truly find the answer he seeks. Tempted by fata morganas, illusions and the fear in his heart - only the stars giving glimpses of truth.

And what about time itself? Watch our story shift to a different time, possibly a time before time itself. Certainly before the past and definitely not what we might call present. And then watch it shift again, just as if the sand makes new shapes as the wind blows through it.

Now you know me as the JESTER but let me put a name to that occupation of the court. My name is Arcadaeus. Me, the one mortal left on this celestial stage!

Oh, poor Arcadaeus - lost on the shores of sand and time! In the heart of the Saharan desert: a place of quest and mystery, the dried up ocean of one's inner journey, just behind the shoals of disbelief or what we thespians call the curtain. But now abandoned by the panthenon, all patrons of the actor's stage and play.
The crowds have long moved on to other plains, their nomad sails are merely shimmering on the horizon, over sunken cities, buried stone.

Oh, poor Arcadaeus - the last to know what once was home: the kingdom of the king of old. Of life and love and dreams of hope - that's what my humble story told, but even then the rulers of the throne, they only spoke and never listened, but to the stories of their own - perhaps that's when all went wrong.'

He picks up a face mirror and looks into it, gives himself a sigh and pokes his tongue out at his reflection. He tries on a mask. He takes it off and tosses it aside.

'Oh, poor thee, through all their reign - the king and Queen - they never came to me - Arcadaeus for not a smile or a cry. A mere spectacle on that great stage - poor mortal, suffered fool, that's my domain to say.

I'm the director and the host of play - supposed to be the fool that makes the king a boy again to think and feel and change the heart - but pah! those efforts were in vain - lost every thought, every bit - every wit - until the boy ran out of time.

And as for him, the King....long gone his rule and law, the fallen kingdom's wall: bare stones - in ruins, where they stood.
The Halls of Sand and Time - decayed to dust and seconds past: The King boy no more, is now the old fool, that stood before - his sight, the brilliance of his mind turned blind and thus the King that never bowed in youth his hours up side down, now bends and bows - brought to his knees by age and old age's deed. And still he yearns for his Queen.

But as for the Queen, time's not a loyal servant borne: she seeks the life and not the old - forsaken blood and bone. As such unfolds the fortune both of kings and rogues - but remind you not forgotten - NEVER! - is the throne, that knows no colour nor oath, short of his own desire - a ruler cursed to call it home - of young and eager spirit, to claim the kingdoms name, his name, and speak the words which break the spell, that kept the seven gates.

A king to rule the realm of men in passing night - until the day the earth stands still - with every grain of sand that passed the twisting of the hourglass wearing down on the bearing King, and grinding thin the stones and walls - alas the end of one is only a call for those to come: the Knave that wants to mount the throne with colours of blood flying high and clear and brave of heart to challenge time and sand of old and follow once again the path of kings and kingdoms past.'

The JESTER casually turns his attention

Sorry, that was quite a monologue. What do you think about the prose though? Sophisticated or a bit over the top? It's what they call 'court speak'. Pays the rent, well, it used to. Aha, I'll just take a break. Perhaps I'll tone it down later.

For now the JESTER simply watches as events proceed.

The King stirs and shifts his position as if agitated. He surveys the void around him and cries out 'How long have I been asleep again? Cassim! Where are you? How long has it been?' The skeleton on the wall comes clattering to life. The skinny torso that is Cassim rattles into some semblance of life, shakes off the dust and muses the question.

'As long as the last time, oh sire! A precise eternity!'

The King is not amused by this response. He knows Cassim too well and refuses to play his little games. He shouts 'When was the last time I could look upon her face? My Queen! My heart! Cassim, I can't even remember what she looks like. Every memory fainted. When was the last time I've seen her, tell me truthfully?'

Cassim turns his head upwards and gives out a loud sigh. He has heard this question a thousand times before and he responds in a dry, bored voice 'The cursed day you had me prisoned here - and locked away until my flesh would rot and bones be turned to dust. Now, you only have me as company. Shall I rattle my chains for you?'

'Silent, Cassim! I do remember. Was it a dream? I was looking up in the sky. And there she was. A procession of storks flying over the kingdom, as beautiful as a sunrise. It reminded me of the Jasmin blossoming in the garden.
For every year after year. She smiled at me, that's what I remember.'

'Your memory plays tricks on you. A fool's dream, Sire. Nothing blossoms here any more and no sun rises ever again. We're just two souls in purgatory.'

The wind whistles around in the void; the two beings survey each other and grimace, each holding a mutual hate of each other, but at the same time locked together in their separate misery.

The King adjusts his position and plays with a ring on his finger. He strokes his beard and shouts loudly 'You're right - what fate has bestowed upon me - no smile but a cruel smirk. The dead laughing at our ghost that cannot die, nor flee the hands of time.
A better fate if you would've succeeded in life to kill me then, and claim the throne - the curse would be yours!
And I would be again with her, my Queen - free of sand and sorrow.'

Somewhere in the void the wind is replaced by a rustle among the dusty ruins. The King picks up on the change of sound. He is puzzled.

'What is that? The wind, somebody or something moving? Impossible! It must be my thoughts racing on an ill turn! There hasn't been motion in this desert place, since ... well since forever!'

And in the distance measured not in metrics, the sandclock is tipped on its side.

The JESTER speaks.

Funny old thing time…. normally gauged by events, milestones significant dates and so forth. What you humans do when celebrating a birthday, a wedding, a holiday, a funeral and the monthly pay slip, until you retire, and then that itself becomes an event of time significance. Without these occurrences time itself is simply a matter of ageing, of progression, nay even of relativity to other events in physics. And in the known universe only the Earth is able to watch time pass. And as time passes so the Earth grows older. So this planet, more than any other celestial creation has become something of interest to the King. In fact more than just an interest, it's been his obsession for the last 4.5 billion years. He's called it his Queen. Above anything else that exists in the known universe the king has put Earth, quite literally, on the throne.

For the King, well he/it IS time. And time moves on. But in this void where power still has a value and is there to be used and abused and sought after, there is not much to celebrate. He probably doesn't even know how old he is. But the sands shift and power is there for the holding or taking.

Sorry to distract…. oh by the way, they can't hear me….or see me….only you, sorry………

Cassim puts him down with a sarcastic comment about his age and senility. Cassim sees his rival like one would a crusty old chess player, there to be outwitted or outmanoeuvred, but a necessary opponent. He says to the King 'Nothing lasts forever sire, not even eternity!' The King lets forth with a roaring shout 'How do you know what goes on down there? You have no eyes!'

Cassim responds. 'No eyes indeed! Taken by the crows, the last to leave this place, those buggers! But your grace was kind enough to chain me up to these walls to become one with the stone. For now I see, what these walls see and I feel what those stones feel and I endure the weight these pillars bear.'

And the King sends back a volley. 'Spare me your foul quirks, ghoul! Just tell me who it is! Is it my Queen? Is it her? Have you returned, my love?'

And then a passing shot back 'Oh, shut it, you old coot! Even if she walked those ruins, she wouldn't recognize your scraggy gob!'

The JESTER speaks.

30/15 to quote a tennis metaphor!
This is how time passes - a series of digs and japes at each other, relentlessly. It can get a little tedious. But at this precise point there does appear to be something novel occurring. Interesting.

'I could've had your tongue cut out as well! Cassim, tell me I order you. Who is it now?'

Cassim dangles perilously and shakes with a sardonic look. 'A ghost from the land of the living, Sire. A contender! Keen and strong in character and mind! He seeks your throne …' The King hears what is said and butts in 'Oh, let him have it - let him reach the seventh gate. And be done with this curse - let him burn my colours and hoist his. Let him wear my crown and burden. See how it feels for him!'

Cassim is unable to control his glee as he hears the King and throws in a devastating prospect '.. and capture the heart of a Queen.'

The King turns quiet, grinding his jaw in anger. He shrugs off the remark. 'Hah! What of it. He will come no further than the others. Another one that bites the dust.'

'You underestimate the desire of man, your highness. This time, they send their best. An old adversary's pawn ...ambitious for greater things.'

The King spins around and with a tilt of his head he ponders what Cassim has said. 'You say a human contender, but that is impossible, no human can challenge me, the king of time, it is beyond human comprehension, it is contained in the ancient laws and I don't mean those mortal laws of Physics either, you scranny ragged mess. It is buried in the ethereal world too far a distance in time and space for any mortal.'

Right on cue a little fanfare hoots from the forecourt. Again, something of a play on words. It is a vortex of physical will and wind blowing a shrillness which descends into a fart of noise.

Cassim summons a breath and speaks 'His royal lordship, the Knave - conqueror of the four corners of the earth - charmer of the seven seas and ...ruler of the Knights of Red!'

' What sort of title do you call that? A comedy piece if I'm not mistaken. Is he here to entertain me or challenge me?'

A loud yell shrieks outside of the King's domain and the sounds of horses riding at speed can be heard. The King is clearly baffled at this unusual state of affairs.

<<ODE, KING OF KINGS - Ye Mighty hear my call.

I will stand the test of trial - the quest of sand and time! As I have proven worthy stepping up the hidden path to your Kingdom's gated walls! I solicit inspection of me and my men to claim the vacant throne. Thus speaks the Knave, and this is my desire! My time is HERE. The sandclock lies on its side and awaits for one of us to set it up again. Your way or my way?>>

The King walks around, prods Cassim in the ribs and regards him with contempt. He strokes his chin and retorts.

'The Knave? Haven't I been punished enough? From all creatures roaming, he gets to be the one? The rogue of fortune? The assassin butcher, that was sent by you, my so called loyal vizier to chop my head off?'

Cassim cocks his skull to the side and lifts his jaw. 'Pfff, that guy has nerves. He was supposed to deliver you *to*, not *from* the land of the dead. Also, the worst refund policy ever. By god, that was a fortune! And now I'm paying for it.' He lowers his jaw and jabs a bony finger into his ribs.

The King continues to rant to himself.... 'No, no, no - NO! Not to this daemon. If losing her is my destiny, alright I can live with that, but not to him! Not like this.'

He yells out of the window. 'We are closed! Go away!'

The Knave and his six accomplices stand there mounted on their steeds, a little dumbfounded at his reaction. One of them turns whispering to the other.

The JESTER intercedes.

Dumbfounded. Indeed as you may be! So this "Knave" as he calls himself is no mortal being. He has made advances on the kingdom before and, as you may have evinced tried to remove the

King, via Cassim at some earlier point in time. An abject failure it must be said. No, he masquerades as the Knave to give him human form. Other than that, I can't really help you on his precise being.

He knows that the King has taken a significant interest in the workings of the Earth and has, to exploit the King's interest and amplify his anger, used a mortal term to convey his presence. The six accomplices he'd call his knights, but again they are ethereal creatures, celestial, spiritual, what have you. And so the dynamics proceed.

The horses (!) shuffle and spin as the seven work out what is going on. The Knave sends out a laugh and confides in his men.

<<The King has retreated back into his block of sand. Hmm, a castellated move, methinks, if I was to use a chess metaphor. So early on as well. He must sense defeat already>>

The accomplices remain unconvinced by the stillness in the air and lack of any sound from above. One speaks out: They're not letting us in. Are they allowed to do that? I thought those beings were bound to stuff like that? Unlimited power, but surely to play by the rules?

His mate replies: You read too many books - this ghost is still king - why should he be bound to open the gates to his kingdom? I've stood before many kingdom gates - and none of them opened by asking.

Yeah, but those were real kingdoms - we're in the realm of the dead. That is his curse as eternal king. He must accept the challenge. Otherwise how can we get back?

Heavens, my missus is pregnant again - I can't be stuck here!

Bloody hell - your Missus is always pregnant, you being there or not …

The Knave turns around to his men. He's clearly had a bad day of it and shows his lack of patience with the gossip among the six.

<<Stand fast and stop your jaw you bunch of mercenary half wits. The King has no power over the older laws that demand our right for trial. If he wants to play tough to get, so be it. Besides something tells me the trial has already started. The kingdom walls are in ruin - every way inside is as easy as the next. We will make our way through the cistern and climb up the old well. I entered this kingdom before to try to take his life and will do so again to take his throne>>.

He draws his black sword and the mercenaries do it after him.

<<To the cistern cave!>>

They ride off to the flank of the kingdom. Above them the King watches with cold eyes. He turns his attention to Cassim, lowers his voice and utters:
'He failed before, he will fail again. He is not worthy of her - I know men like him.'

Cassim senses his yearning and pain. He responds with a similar touch 'He reminds you of yourself, all those ages ago, doesn't he?'

'Yes, but I changed. Can he? No. He will always be the brute and worse he's not of honour. Tried to stab me while I was asleep. I changed, he will not.'

But now Cassim sees an opportunity to get his own back and changes his attitude. He scowls at the King and pours out his venom and his anger. 'You turned weak. That's why the cleric turned against you, but if it is of any consolation - my contract with the Knave involved painless poisoning.'

'How kind of you, Vizier. And fitting for a spineless snake.'

Cassim finds the opportunity to change his tack and now plays with the King. 'Hmm, the daily business of politics. You've never had a problem turning a blind eye on my methods, as long as they favoured you. But I wonder - you never told me - what exactly happened on the night that the Knave came to assassinate you? He wasn't the one that attempted that act, was he?'

'No Cassim, some things even surpass the eye of the wall unseen. I dare say you know the answer to your own question? Reveal, you rotten corpse.'

Above them the JESTER begins to follow the trail of the Knave by jumping from roof to roof. Sand and dust filter down. The Knave seems familiar with the territory and is able to navigate the warrens and many side streets before him.

The JESTER speaks

Ah love, the only thing shared by the living and the dead. Two nobles, the future and the king of past battling over who's to last. An adventure of the noble knight? How uninspiring - yes, alright ...
But then - what of it, you might ask? The Knave - just an upstart, another sand of grain that falls?

Not worthy of our time and hearts, just put before the reaper - flailed and threshed and pulled apart and neatly stacked?

But that's not where the story goes - no, that's just skirmish as you know - a hero at the very start is not a hero yet at all - the tale still has to find that diamond in the rough, without it's shining armour, pure - uncut.

But before we turn to such endeavour - one of the divine still has to enter the stage of the kingdom now: the love of kings - blossom of the jasmin's spring, fulfilling every tear and dream: the living spirit of the DESERT Queen!

CHAPTER 4

CONFRONTATION

In Northern Italy, Padre Alfonso's sister and brother in law had been celebrating their 45th wedding anniversary in a village near Bergamo. In the middle of the night Guiseppe was admitted to the local hospital following several days of a high temperature, a dry cough and breathing difficulties. He died 2 days later. It was the 20th of February 2020. 3 days previously Italy had declared a state of emergency, the first country in Europe to respond so dramatically to the events that were once 'China's problem.'   2 days after that, on the night of the 25th February Guiseppe's wife went to sleep and never woke up. She had overdosed on medication to alleviate her anxieties following the death of her husband. She was 71 years of age.

When Padre Alfonso received the news, via his other sister, he was overwrought with grief. He had been aware that there seemed to be an outbreak of the virus in the north, but wasn't prepared for the agonising news that came with it. He felt an overwhelming urgency to rewrite his Sunday sermon, though he thought that it may have to be put back if he had to travel up to the region for the funeral.

However, by the end of February, 29 people had died in the region with numbers rising at an alarming rate. It was too dangerous to travel. Alfonso would never attend his late sister and brother in law's funeral.

The sermon would go ahead. Naples would never forget it.

Sunday morning the 2nd March came with a chilly wind and a hint of rain. The tourist coaches had yet to arrive and the cafes would open in about an hour. A few scrawny cats chased around the entrance to Padre Alfonso's church as the bells called in the faithful. This morning though, unusually, Padre Alfonso was not greeting his flock at the door and the few dozen members of the church proceeded in and took their place in the cold and dank of its interior. A few started chatting about events near and far as they looked in the service book for the beginning of today's service and opening hymn. The service started on cue at 9.30 and Padre Alfonso walked into the sanctuary. He was on his own. Again this was unusual as he would normally have two altar boys with him swinging the incense lamps. A few members of the congregation whispered. He continued the service and spoke the liturgy. Then came the sermon.

'One month ago my children, I preached to you about the value of sacrifice. I preached to you about the way our lord withstood the pain and the temptation and how his ultimate triumph was to see god from the cross and conquer sin. Today my sermon looks back on that theme……. you see we are all sinners before god, but we have a choice, to give in to sin or to fight it, and in so doing we must make a sacrifice. But the temptations of Lucifer are strong as I'm sure some of you already know.

Those of you who choose to sleep with your own kind, those of you who choose to allow your unborn to die, those of you who in your ageing would quietly wish you could determine your own life or death. I say unto you. You have been shown the true path yet you ignore and choose the easy road, the road that you believe is your free will over your body. It is not how our lord wants it. I am a humble padre and I have taken my vows in the belief that I walk the true path. I will no longer welcome the sinners into my flock. Time after time you, and you know who you are, take the

easy way. Be gone.

Thus spake Ezekiel···

> The path of the righteous man is beset on all sides by the inequities of the selfish and the tyranny of evil men. Blessed is he who, in the name of charity and good will, shepherds the weak through the valley of darkness, for he is truly his brother's keeper and the finder of lost children. And I will strike down upon thee with great vengeance and furious anger those who attempt to poison and destroy my brothers. And you will know my name is the Lord when I lay my vengeance upon thee.

So do I shed my blood for you and all you do is spite me.'

And with that Padre Alfonso took a long sharpened nail from his cassock and with his left hand

proceeded to push the nail into the palm of his right hand. He lifted his bloodied hand up to show

the congregation. There were loud audible screams from the pews as Padre Alfonso passed out on

the marble floor.

When he came around two minutes later a few of his faithful had gathered around him. By chance

a first aider was attending, some tourist from Bari in the south and she had loosened his collars. His

hand was bandaged. He was told he'd need a Tetanus jab and should see a doctor; one of the

congregation said he needed to see a shrink and was going to write to the cardinal, worrying

everyone like that, what a way to behave.

Padre Alfonso found it difficult to sleep that evening. The world somehow seemed a scary place and

he was worried that those voices would return. Which they did. That night.

He awoke from a very restless night having snatched at most two hours sleep. Padre Alfonso was

not looking forward to the day ahead.

....

Pablo Mendes, the city councillor, was becoming more concerned. He was convinced that he had been followed one previous Sunday after mass and that he was about to be exposed. Events in Bogota were warming up and it seemed that the authorities were becoming very intolerant to low level crime and drugs and prostitution rackets: no doubt with the elections coming up and promises to clean the streets for the tourist year ahead. The press had also latched onto the crime rate as a moral panic. Even though the big organaised crime gangs had either been arrested or gone to ground, the press was shouting out for more blood and calling on the polticians to earn their keep. Renata was aware that Pablo was particularly edgy and went off running a few errands when he demanded to see all the daily papers. Nothing, so far. Neverthless, he spoke with his henchmen and told them to keep a watch and an ear open to anything going on that might cause alarm.

Mendes continued his uncertainties and anxiety when he went into the bedroom and unlocked the smaller of two wardrobes. He looked inside and made a mental note of the contents. The church he visited was a trusting church but there were limits: it did not want to see the altar silver go walkabouts, especially given the poverty of the congregation. So Pablo Mendes, so called loyal worshipper and 'man of the people' public servant, was entrusted to keep it safe. But he failed to tell the church elders that it was stashed in his wardrobe and they didn't ask questions. He reflected, counted the silver again and thought 'well, you never know, just in case of a rainy day.' Behind him, Renata had been standing by the bedroom door all along. She took a sneak photograph on her cellphone and quietly retreated back into the kitchen.

Time to get your own back, thought Renata.

Two days later the Bogota Post ran with a page 3 article. **"Pablo the Silver Thief?"** The article, and a photograph suggested that Pablo Mendes, a city councillor of many years standing was embezzling the local catholic church of its riches. Mendes saw the article and was livid. Either the paparazzi had an extremely powerful camera lens or it was his wife. But he had to fix the press first. He rung his lawyer down town and told him to shut the press up or he'd be suing for defamation.

He stormed back onto the verandah and confronted his wife. Renata knew what to expect but this time she was no longer the timid defensive housewife. When he accused her of attempting to ruin his public life she just let it all out. 'That's just a start you son of a bitch. I know what you do after mass on a Sunday afternoon. I know why we live the life we do on a politician's allowance. Right now my lawyer, yes, my lawyer…..didn't even know I had one did you…..and he's free of your corruption….. will be putting a letter in his safe, to be opened if anything sudden and unusual happens to me. He has been instructed to send it to the Bogota Post where they will certainly print the contents. You need to reign yourself in and start behaving…..Oh, and just for your information, you know that TV series you enjoy watching… well maybe you think yourself the new godfather, but right now I AM THE ONE WHO KNOCKS.'

…………………………………………………..

Rick went over to Phil's place to play some dystopian zombie attack game on the Nintendo.They started to discuss the state of the blog and some of the issues they were covering. Rick chips in 'We should take a break, somewhere hot, get away from this bloody rain and cold. I haven't had a holiday since last year and I could probably wangle and fortnight out of the boss. We could do a bit of blogging from our hotel blah blah blah, whatever, so yeah, whdya think Phil. Give the blog a whole new feature…. poiltical meltdown in Egypt or summing, what they don't tell you about the Lebanon, corrupt politicians, I dunno. Just a thought.'

Phil turned to Rick. 'You plan it then pal. You give me an idea where to go, prices, flights and I'll see. Now, concentrate on this zombie that's wielding an axe to your head, you're losing big time.'

Three hours later and half a dozen zombies down, Rick and Phil decided to call it an evening. Phil picked up on the earlier conversation. 'You serious about going to the middle east then? I'm up for it, don't have to think about time off. I like the idea of giving the blog a new twist; I've been watching the markets and there seems to be a big interest in some oil that's unique to Morocco, actually around the south, Marrakesh area. Called Argan oil I think. Not sure why the interest has taken off now though, wouldn't mind doing a bit of digging around. What about we go to Morocco. Only about 4 hours flight, possibly from Bristol airport?' Rick nodded an approval. 'Sure thing man.'

…………………………………………

Gabriella arrived at the rail station in Madrid. She had left Seville that morning following a blazing row with Jose. It hadn't been a picture book Christmas for them and the new year didn't start off much better either. She hated the coat he had bought her, but conceded that it would do for the trip to Madrid. And damn it, she'd made the emotional investment in buying him a ring. That says something. Coat, huh. Cheapskate. But something didn't feel right. It turned and turned in her head for most of the journey. In Madrid it had been raining and the clouds still lingered. It all looked a bit grey. She hailed down a taxi. 'To the Fama Agencia, Avenida dela Institucion de Ensenanza, prego'.

She arrived at the modelling studio. It was a little disappointing: not some glamorous fronted building with the neon signs she expected. It was set on the second floor above a estate agent office. She pressed the buzzer. An anonymous voice asked for some ID. The buzzer made a sharp click and she opened the door and walked the floor to the studio front door. Hmm, understated place, she thought. Not quite the studio she had in mind.

Gabriella was welcomed by a guy who called himself Ernesto. He introduced himself as the agent who would go through the details of a potential modelling contract with photo opportunities. In the room she could see a couple of white unbrellas, the kind you get at a photo shoot, a large back screen and a few props lying around on the floor. To the front of all this was a camera on a tripod.

'So, Gabrielle, Gabriella, sorry. My job is to take a few photos and submit them to my boss, he's away at the moment doing a magazine photoshoot over in San Sebastian. Won't be back for a few days. If he likes you he'll make contact with me and I'll take things to the next step.' Gabriella took this in with an appealing smile. 'So, have you done much modelling?' Gabriella told him about some of her earlier work, upped it all a bit for effect. Ernesto wasn't taking any notes but just nodded. 'Great. So now, we do a little photography yes. If you could stand over there in front of the screen. Great. OK, let me set up the camera. Now, OK, look at the camera, let me see a few positions, hand on hip, yes, oh, that's good yes. Other hand. Good. Maybe the left hand and arm brushing back your hair, OK. Maybe seated now. OK, so legs crossed, good, legs out…. a little more, don't be shy. OK good. OK, so now please can you take off your top. Is that OK? You can leave your bra on. I know, but the boss will want to see how you look if there's a clothes modelling deal. OK, so to the left, maybe put your hand on the left boob, pout. Great. OK, now your jeans off please.' Click, click, click.

…………………………………………………………..

January was a slow month in the hospitality industry. All that Christmas food and all the expensive presents, not to mention the excess of alcohol. No money and a few weeks to wait until the January salary went into the bank, around the 27-28 of the month. Alain was bored stiff. Some of the staff had been laid off so he was working with just a few co-workers and they didn't have their heart in it. January was that kind of month. Grin and bear it and hope you still had a job in February, even in a Michelin starred restaurant. But Alain had decided he had enough of it.

He had submitted his CV to the local college and had been shortlisted for interview. He was confident his reputation in the industry would speak for itself and felt that he would have a good chance of being offered the position. But he wasn't going to assume anything. He went out and bought a suit. That itself wasn't so easy. He had to find a specialist tailor in Lyons which catered for his XXL size. Eventually he managed to get something suitable but he had to pay more than he wanted. He hoped that his weight would not be a hindrance, though he had to admit it was something he should sort out. Too much snacking and duff food.

The interview was scheduled for a Tuesday morning, mid January. If he was successful, he would need to give two weeks notice to the restaurant and start beginning February. He appeared before 3 people on the panel who all asked a few questions about his background, in turn. Alain took them through his CV and sidestepped one or two questions about his "management style". 45 minutes later he was out and heading back to his flat.

He got a call later that afternoon. He listened to the call….the good news…. we'd like to offer you a position within the college, starting the beginning of February. It's a permanent part time position, 20 hours a week. Alain quizzed them about the full time post also on offer, but apparently that had gone to an internal candidate. Would he take the offer? Alain cursed to himself under his breath, rolled his eyes and said 'Yes, I'd love to take your offer.' The conversation, from the college end, mostly focussed on a few bits of information about giving notice and picking up an ID badge and induction details. When Alain eventually put the phone down he drew a sigh and shouted 'Bollocks' very loudly. This isn't how it was supposed to go, he thought. But he was not going back to that restaurant, so maybe this would be a stop gap as he looked and decided as to where he should go. Yes, treat this as a temporary manoeuvre.

His neighbour knocked on his door and asked if she could walk the dog. Alain called her in. 'Monique, I know you like walking the pooch and how it helps you with your anxiety and whatever. And I'm grateful you have been doing this to help out when I'm on shift. But I was stopped last week while out walking him by someone who said they recognised the dog, or one very similar and thought it belonged to an elderly lady. Is that you by any chance? Because walking the dog is one thing, but telling people it's yours is another.' The neighbour tensed up and burst into tears, but Alain wasn't the type to empathise with people suffering a mental health issue. 'OK stop crying. I've got a new job starting in February so we'll have to see how things go. Come around in half an hour, I need to feed her first.'

………………………………………………..

Katrin received a letter from Sven two weeks after he had left Stuttgart to join an NGO in Mozambique. The letter was pretty depressing with references to food shortages and disease, minor corruption among the police and public services and concerns over the date of the next large food donation from Oxfam and the African wing of UNICEF. He said in his letter that he was hoping to get some time off at the end of February to fly back for a break and maybe Katrin could organise a trip away for them both. Katrin didn't think much of it at first and had returned to work with a pressing schedule of contracts and designs to kick start and sign off. However, by the end of the third week of January thoughts of her time in Morocco returned and wouldn't go away. She'd heard an interview featuring members of Led Zeppelin and at one point they were talking about the inspiration for the number 'Kashmir', it being the sounds and harmonies of North African music, inspired by a visit to, none other than Marrakesh.

They had to go. She sent Sven a text message saying she was going to investigate a short, 6-7 day break to Marrakesh in early March. Two days later she received a reply to say go ahead, find something. Katrin wasted no time and checked some local flights on the few budget airlines available in Germany. Decent money 85 euro each way ex Munich. She checked a few sites for riads in Marrakesh and took a screen shot of a couple of awesome photos to send to Sven. At the same time she checked with her line manager whether there was any need to do any chasing up on the deal she had commissioned back in 2019, in Agadir. No, nothing needed. Pity she thought, could have possibly fitted in a short business trip with a little RnR in Marrakesh. Oh well, the trip wouldn't cost a fortune and it would be a little tick on the 'must do before I die' list. She resumed her work on the company laptop, plugged in her earphones and found a Kraftwerk album to settle into.

CHAPTER 5

GAME PLAN

Having spent some time and considerable energy going through the warren that is the Kings domain the Knave and his accomplices enter the vast, fortified, cistern chamber through a crack not wide enough for the horses. The cistern cave lies in empty darkness, the only light shining through a hole in the ceiling. There is a single rope dangling from the hole, just slightly out of one's reach. The Knave takes off his blackened helmet, sweat running from his brows. He makes a quarter turn, to face out - breaking the fourth wall. He gives a regal wave of contact.

<<What? Hellooo....

Oh, you thought only the JESTER was able to speak with you? Only he was allowed to do that? Such privilege. Nay, you must be my witness. Let me speak openly. I'll not take up too much of your time, if you'll excuse the pun. Time, time, tic toc tic.

Call me far sighted, but the old order is dead. You see, the passage of time brings with it too many uncertainties. Where is it going, who is going with it, what will it all look like? Nah.....

Come on, no-one wants that much uncertainty. Since time began I have tried to control its trajectory. But, I've got to say, it's been a struggle. It's a tall order for one celestial being to do it all on ones own.

Man came a long way! Didn't he just! Yes, OK, granted, the human was an evolution of this time, no-one could have predicted it - and boy, was it hard going getting this far!

From flint and fire, to crossing oceans to reach for the stars: capable of such manipulation, oh my!

Oh, I've not mentioned it have I? Me, moi, The Knave, the future king, that's me friends. I that has brought the human to where we are now, not mother earth. No doubt she'll say she had the upper hand in it…but……left to her they'd still be crawling around on all 4's wondering what to do with an animal bone and sniffing each other's arse.

So I played a few hands and made a few moves to bring us to here. This place. This time.

You may wonder why earth seems to be struggling with unusual forces of late … plagues, disasters, exodus, confusion and a breakdown in old certainties.

Not haphazard, not natural forces, no sir, tis she! She wishes to restore the "balance". But the balance brings into play all sorts of problems. Like uncertainty. You want uncertainty? You want chaos? No, you don't.

You want a sense of ORDER. No more of the uncertainties of time, bring on the certainty of time repeating itself, forever.

That's what I came for: to slay the dragon, that holds the maidens heart.

Hmm, I like that: to - slay - the - dragon.   What I really mean is that I want HER off the board.

And by the way, I've moderated my language quite a bit, so far. Early days, don't want to give too much away this far into the game. I want to see how the King responds.

Watch out for things to happen. Suspend your disbelief, it's going to be a bugger of a ride>>

The Knave leads his band of outlaws into the centre of the cistern, but as they step forward they start to sink into the sand. Ignoring any obstacle he pushes on, locked on his target - to reach the rope. The accomplices do not dare to fall behind, but fear is growing among them. Until one of them speaks of what is becoming obvious.

The ground is not safe, my liege! We should stop and consider our plan!

<<Be silent, coward! Of course they test us! Our sheer will and heart! It is the one that doesn't stop - no matter the cost ... mmfffggghh, oh, the stench>>

The troop is now already waist high stuck, just a few steps away from the rope. But within seconds the troop find themselves in difficulties and, stuck up to the nostrils are unable to move.

<<Hrfmfmgfgg. Shit, this place stinks>>

Suddenly a strong wind is blowing. And the crystal clear laugh of a woman is echoing through the cave. Near suffocation the Knave forces his eyes open one more time.

The most beautiful of faces comes close to his. The DESERT Queen walking over the quicksand without even leaving a trace. It's as if she is gliding on air and the method to her freedom and elegance is in sharp contrast to that of The Knave and his troop, who are all struggling to keep above the foulness and breathe.

'Shhhhh. Time to catch your breath - there is nothing to hurry if you walk upon quicksand!
Oops, did I tell you that too late? Hahahaha! No, don't look at me like that, look at you - such a shame for such a handsome face - I could get used to those lips and piercing eyes.
What fire, what youth! What a pity you pretty boys are always as dumb as a knob. Heading in so light-headed and then hitting rock-bottom and sinking like a stone. You are probably now wondering how deep this pit goes?
Well - to make a long answer short - from the bottom of the upper lip, all the way down to your toes.

Just enough to separate the wheat from the chaff. A good height may suffice to save.

Ah, where is my hero? If even one of you would at least make beyond the first gate. I should perhaps change my hopes - or lower my standards. Even a Queen is allowed to reminisce about her king of passed time.'

The Queen turns her sight to the rope hanging from the well above and the eyes of the Knave follow.

'Think you can make it Knave?'

<<Hhhgmmmhhmm. So this is how you'll end my ambition, tired old Earth. I don't think so… your time is over, look at the evidence. It's all around for you to see. Decay, disillusion and indifference pervades the place>>

'No, don't make yourself hope. You will die in here, Knave. Did you really think you would be worth a Queen? What fool men are.'

She playfully tips the end of the dangling rope.

'The thread of fate. An eternity in one state or another. 4.54 billion years as it is fashion to believe right now.

Or, if you're more into your stories of old: Seven Days.

I have seen many changes. I have witnessed evolution. From the storms and radiance of the heavens to the cold and icy extremities of my dominion. From ice caps being created to ice caps melting. From volcanic eruption and tsunami.

And I have even taking the punches of meteorites, from dust to dust - so called heavenly bodies from outer space. There was a big one, about 70 million years ago, my that rocked the boat. Changed the order of things, oh my. But, out of my control and not my domain to say, strictly off limits.

As I revolve in space , my fate is determined by the passage of time and the vagaries of a solar system. Or so I thought. That is the law of physics is it not?

The womb of chaos, that brought all life into being? But No.

No longer am I Queen of all I contain. No longer am I in control. That luxury has been slowly slipping from my grasp over the time of humankind and its evolution!

All things must pass. But No.

Synchronicity is moving ever further away. Stop, I hear you cry. You are yearning for a time passed, a reminiscence for the old order. But No.

How can I put this to you. You, hanging for your life in the lavatory of the cesspool, you who would try to usurp the natural order and also you, mortal reader?

You will no doubt know time as the progression of events from the past to the present into the future.

It is not something we can see, touch, or taste, but we can measure its passage.

I have seen its passage. 4.54 billion years.

You want to change the order of things. You, Knave. And the humans. Just 3 million of my years. By now turning the sand clock on its head, putting the future before the past: Putting order before chaos.

Oh, I get it from your perspective - in the centre of the sand clock: the present, where all is in harmony.

The calm in the middle of the storm. Or so it was. Until I sensed a disturbance:

Men mounting their campaign to change the world order. The sand-clock is to be turned upside down, again and again, so that the past, becomes the future, forever. Thus I was taken, imprisoned, taken off the board so to speak. But I know the way back. My huntsmen, even now will conspire a strategy.

You have prisoned me long enough - but I will be prisoned no longer, Knave! Your orderly circle ends here with you. I have other plans and once you've failed I'm free!

So spare with me, when I don't wish you any luck, but a quick death! I shall be free of all men.

Well , I'll see you on the other side.'

And with that the desert Queen is gone.

The Knave stares into the blank. His brow is revolting in ambition. He cannot move forward, but he gets his arm out of the quicksand - reaching up.

The rope is way out of his reach.

He harrumphs once again, reaching for his last strength and instead of trying to grab the rope he pushes himself on to the back of one of his acolytes. A mere pawn in the long game.

Sacrificing the man he climbs, until he stands on the shoulders of a second. He too succumbs to the weight. He cries out in pain, then silence.

<<Ah, 2 pawns down but plenty left to take on a withered old king>>, muses the Knave.

He grabs the rope and starts climbing up the well.

<<She has made her move. I WILL MAKE MINE. One move nearer to conquest>>

CHAPTER 6

DISAPPOINTMENT

As January came to an end Pablo Mendes had decided that his illicit side-business in Bogota needed to be wound up. He paid off his henchmen with sufficient consideration and an assurance that they would keep secrets safe. The hookers were dispensable and would have to make their own future out of whatever was left in them that could command payment. But the politician was looking a long way over the water for his next enterprise. Get out of Colombia. He had left Renata and the children. There was no future in it, too many threats and insufficient power to rally against it. A decent financial arrangement and a visit every third Saturday to see the kids. That was the best he could get. And eternally damned by her family.

The city paper was sniffing around, he knew it and it was only a matter of time before the whole sordid world of his corruption would be public for the masses to hit on. Colombians were not known for forgiveness despite their christian lifeblood, so he had to make things look good. Then get out of the place. Maybe settle in Argentina, who knows.

But for now, a little rookie business in a place called Thailand. Thai brides, massage parlours, erotic clubs. Enormous opportunity and it was a free market as well. Lots of small private entreprenneurs but no security, no overlord to offer protection. Mendes could see a nice little earner far away from the Bogota Post and the journalists who wanted to see him behind bars, or maybe even cemented into some office block development. He made a few calls and arranged an appointment with a Mr Lu, some minor heavyweight in Bangkok who apparently knew a few people he could negotiate with. Mendes wasn't slow to ask if Mr Lu could arrange a meet up with a couple of young Thai girls, of legal age, of course, that he could hire to escort him around the tourist and red light hot spots. No problem.

………………………………….

Gabriella convinced herself she had done the right thing. I'm a professional after all, she reflected on herself. She didn't feel anything for Ernesto and that was the main thing wasn't it? OK, so he needed to see her modelling nude, well that's what professional models have to do. It's all part of the portfolio. And when he suggested she stay over and maybe do another shoot the following day, well that was good fortune, more opportunity, wasn't it? He was gentle enough and the two bottles of Rioja and a Cava did wonders to ease the whole thing. Still, best not to mention it to Jose, he wouldn't understand.

Ernesto said he was quite pleased with the photos and would pass them on. He was sure there would be some work as a result. She swore to herself she must never say a thing to Anna. Gabriella boarded the train back to Seville and started to work out a story to tell Jose for why she took two days away rather than the one.

For the next fortnight Gabriella was hooked to her moible phone and, when home, her landline. Jose was at the receiving end of all her anxieties and fits of depression. "Ernesto, you bastard" she muttered under her breath as she gave up all hope of a modelling career and the front page of Spanish Vogue.

………………………………….

"Corruption at the very heart of the Bogota city administration", ran the Bogota Post. Time was very much running out. And to make matters worse, some of the competition in Mendes life of crime were asking questions and considering options if Mendes ever thought of squealing in return for a get out of jail pass. Mendes checked out flight times to Bangkok at a local travel agent and made the very necessary arrangements to get out of the city. He would lie low in the far east and hoped that the extradition laws, if there were any, didn't cover embezzlement and drug supply.

…………………………………………

Never trust Rick. After all the hype and bullshit he had decided to pull out of any trip to Northern Africa. They'd planned the details immaculately and to the last minute he'd shown nothing but energy and commitment. And now this….. in a text of all things:

> 'Sorry man, I can't go to Morocco. Thought about it but ain't got the 'ackers mate. You go, get the story. Publish and be damned. I'll drive you to the airport though. Cheers.'

Phil just looked at the text, speechless. *"You gonna tell him what you think of him?"* a voice in his head said. "No, can't be bothered". *"Coward"*.

……………………………………………..

There had been a major environmental disater in Bangladesh. Massive flooding along the Ganges had left hundreds of thousands of people homeless and prone to airborne diseases. Aid agencies from across the world were mobilised. Sven packed his bags for the nine hour flight to Kolkata and from there by road to Dacca. He was mentally and physically prepared. He sent a text to Katrin.

Katrin half expected this to happen. Her logical side took the news on the chin but it was how she felt that mattered. Her heart sunk. She had been looking forward to the sun and the colours of Marrakesh and its surroundings. Just a short break. "C'mon Sven. I needed that break."

CHAPTER 7

CONNECTIONS

The King is agitated. 'Cassim! Tell me, what happened? I can feel her presence! But what in the name of all that stinks is that smell?'

Cassim, having no nose to speak off is non plussed by this remark. But he knows what is happening. He throws a comment towards the King. 'Up your shaft: the Knave made his way past the first gate into the Kingdom.Through the shitter.'

'What, that creature from the lowest sink! I've should've known it! Cassim, I cannot let him get through to her! Let me be cursed into hell for eternity again, I will not leave her to him! I'd rather break the wheel of fate and shatter the glass of time, myself! He shall not pass! And why does he even bother the challenge. It is not at all clear what his strategy is. As if there is anything left to seize.....!'

Cassim feels the old King's pain. 'I don't want to spoil your wrath, sire - but that is the rule of the game. And I'm not surprised he's keeping things close to his chest. No-one would give away their game plan so early, and.....his move ...was legit. Though I think he may have sacrificed 2 pieces along the way.'

The King starts to pace hurriedly and strokes his face. He's faced worse in his long existence but Cassim is surprised that he is showing so much anxiety. He shouts. 'I know that. But haven't you been the greatest cheater of all games. There was no loophole in life untested by your deviousness, don't tell me there isn't one now!

Think, Cassim! Let your mischievous spirits wreak havoc one more time. Help me stop him - and I swear by my love - that I will finally see your debt fulfilled and release you.'

'Ah, as if. Don't give me hope, where no hope is, Sire. This game is not prone to mortal tricks and cheatery!' He ponders a little and blows some sand off his shackles and thinks.

'... but maybe we don't have to cheat.'

'What do you mean?'

'Sire, there is no rule on how many can play that game. If it is only the Knave you want to fail, perhaps you could find a better party, worthy of her.'

'And who should that be?'

'One approved by fate, one of chaos: A random choice, to belay the force. A throw of dice so to speak.'

'And where would I get this dice to throw?'

'Sire, you're still the KING OF SAND AND TIME. Use your powers to summon them. Seven strangers against the seven orders: the Knave and his six knights or whatever he prefers to call them ...... well, technically only 4 now - but he is one move ahead - so you get the idea.'

The King glowers and seethes under his breath.' Cassim, stop playing with me and causing me more agony. My powers are limited to the plain of the desert. Of SAND, Cassim! Not living flesh and soul.'

'You really haven't been out lately. Time inside your kingdom has nearly stopped to a trickle of its flow - but time outside has been racing ever since. Faster and faster. Machines now replace the beating heart. Sand has manifested in the pockets of the living. A mirrored throne of sand and time called silicon and byte, pocket sized and with a crystal tower controlling thought and mind. The all-seeing Cyclops. It's big bucks sire!

Chips, they call it: the heart of the machine. But it is nothing more than dreams and sleepy dust.

Now it's time to wake them up. You sire....'

The King shrugs resignedly and faces Cassim. He feels the weight of time and space is against him.

'Pah, what ever it takes - I'm willing to comply. So be it.'

He walks to the centre of the tower spire, crumbling before his eyes. Raising his arms towards the skies he cries out:

SPIRITS OF THE AETHER REALM! HEAR MY COMMAND OF SAND AND TIME. MANIFEST IN GRAIN AND MATTER - CRYSTAL SPHERE: I SUMMON THOSE - FROM CHAOS BOUND - SEVEN OF THE LIVING SOULS!

Thunder growls in the distance. There is movement and a shaking. Dust and sand slip and the castle, or what there is of it, shifts visibly. The King retires.

The JESTER speaks

Hmmm, the King makes his move. I conceive of a cunning plan. Time shifts, the planets turn..and something extraordinary has happened. In the Sahara. For the first time in a thousand years - it rained. And a few thousand miles away, people were interested……..Yes mortals, the game has truly begun.

CHAPTER 8

A CALL TO 7

1   Boston. USA.

The BUSINESSMAN. Seated at his desk. He speaks in his mobile phone.

'You want me to travel to Morocco? Since when did we do business with Morocco?

Oh, right, we' ve, you' ve, started a dialogue with a businessman concerning worldwide sales of a

rare oil, peculiar and unique to the region.

Pause

Could be lots of investment opportunities. Right. Well it' s my area. Sure, I' ll do it.

Pause

Ok, so have you got my plane ticket? Business class of course. Ex JFK?

Pause

Who am I flying with?

Pause

OK. So it' s to Marrakesh. I' ll also need an executive lounge pass for Charles de Gaulle if I' m laying

over for 4 hours.

How long am I over there?

Pause

7 days, enough time for a little RnR?

Which hotel am I booked into? Can I suggest the Radisson in Marrakesh. It's the best in the corporate sector. Have you booked transport?

Pause

I'll get my secretary to book me in, might take a couple of days out to visit the souks and maybe Casablanca.

Send me the details. Thanks Oscar. We'll have to have dinner sometime. I'll speak with Rachel and sort out an evening with you and Marie.

Pause

How are things with that Logistics company? You know, the one we foreclosed on?

Pause

Yes that one. They defaulted on monthly payments, remember?

Pause

Oh, they've gone into liquidation. Serves them right. Far too ambitious. Never kept their eye on the bottom line, Oscar.

Pause

And you. Bye for now. I'll email you after I meet up with this guy in Marrakesh.

He places his mobile mobile on a nearby desk.

Rach, honey, I'm flying out to Marrakesh, that's in Morocco honey. Next week. Business trip. The boss has set up a meeting with some A-rab businessman concerning some unique oil called argon, or aragan, I don't know, but some investment oppo. And he thinks I'm the man to make the deal.

I'll make the usual travel claims. Should be a nice little earner, honey. You wanted a new fridge freezer. Think I'll be able to rustle up something. If I know those A-rabs I can probably negotiate a few "foreigners" ha ha. How about a couple of berber rugs to go in the lounge? I'll sort it.'

………………………………….

2   Lyon, France.

The CHEF. He sits at home. On his own. Watching TV. Eating pizza and a beer. Talks to himself. Feeds his dog a piece of pizza. Then licks his fingers.

'Shit, so much for a fortnight of gourmet food tasting in SE Asia. 87 confirmed cases in Thailand, 43 in Malaysia and Singapore threatening to go into lockdown. Aieeee! Bloody Chinese virus. And I booked this back in October.

Right. Well I've booked 14 days leave and 14 days leave I'm taking. I'll have to be less adventurous. The college can go do one while I'm away. I'm only part time, so they can suck it.

Going to have to try for a refund on that flight. Lucky I didn't pay in advance for all those hotels and the food tasting tours. This isn't going to pad out well.

He picks up a travel brochure.

Tunisia. Nah. Too close to Egypt. Not risking the middle east. I'll get the runs.

Cyprus..... hmm maybe, nice food, lebanese style, hummus, falafel.... maybe not. The Canaries. Come on Alain, shite cuisine, too many Europeans. And I don' t do beach holidays. Morocco. Let' s see.....

He reads from the brochure.

Explore a world of mystery and magic, of souks and markets, of rugs and trinkets. Lose yourself in a land that continues to magnify its colourful past. Walk in the time of the ancient ones and let your taste buds be overcome by the herbs and spices of this welcoming country. Why not take a tour to the sahara and visit the Morocco of old, in a Bedouin tent with camels and gentle drumming Arab music around the sunset fire. Immerse yourself in the culture.
No visa needed!

Yeah, it' ll do. I' ll have to book this quickly before everyone wakes up to the fact that SE Asia is going to be a no go zone for a while.

Flight to.....Marrakesh....check out Bookmyflight....

5 days hotel in the city........max 70 euro per night, need to have dinner and breakfast

3 day Sahara trek....about 100 euro... no way am I doing that, far too much effort and I can' t see any camel taking my gut at the moment.
Maybe a trip to the coast. Essoiura looks good. Very Hipster. Maybe do some Game of Thrones tours around there. No beach sports. Bugger that. Nice restaurants. 2 nights there.
Not quite what I had in mind. Still. Thailand can wait. Doggo, I' m off to North Africa and you' re in kennels.'

3   Naples, Italy

The PADRE. Standing.

He reads a letter....

From Bishop Emilio

Padre, I write this letter with some trepidation and concern for your spiritual health. I think perhaps you should take a few days of leave. I understand the difficulties that are being faced in the north and fully sympathise with your family circumstances. I am sorry for the loss of your brother and sister in Parma and this awful fever is a spiritual challenge to us all. I pray for their souls and their journey to our lord. Recuiesat in pace. But you know that you cannot travel to the North. It is too risky.

Mindful of the concerns of your congregation following your outbursts last Sunday and of late, I urge you to take a little time to rest and reflect on your calling to the lord. Perhaps the weight of your calling has been too much of late. Perhaps I missed the signs as your mentor. Some years ago I visited the beautiful country of Morocco. The country is developing and is quite a haven for tourists. A very beautiful country. I went into the desert for a couple of days and found the experience a wonderful way to reflect on the duties and wonders of our relationship with the Christ Jesus. Pax Vobiscum.

I think a similar visit may help you to both rest and recharge your spirit. I will send on details in the post. Accipe bonum consilium meum.

The Padre throws down the letter.

'Pah, what does he know of struggle? Born into a high class family. Studied at the Sapenzia University of Rome. Elevated to Bishop at the age of 53 . He doesn't even know my brother from my brother in law.

And I. 63 years old and still preaching compassion, love and repentance to a dwindling congregation.

The world has gone mad. Same sex relationships, abortion, love of money, corrupt politicians.

And now the fever. God in his revenge? But why my family? What have I ever done but follow your teachings? How can I sit easily alongside your compassion for the sinner yet watch you take away my bloodline? Why has Berlusconi, not become a victim of this 'great leveller disease' ? Tell me God, tell me in a way I can understand and believe.

And so, to Morocco. 7 days in the heat. Like our saviour. Oh, but he went there for a lot longer.What else have I but my church, what choice do I have? Yes Bishop Emilio. I will go to Morocco. I will take your dictat. But not on your terms.'

....

4   Bristol UK...

The BLOGGER. Sits at home and spends most of his day on social media, thinks himself a 'social influencer.' He is scruffy, wearing his pyjamas and eating a bowl of cereal.

He types into his mobile/tablet.

Strange things happening in Africa. Unusual disturbances not easily explained by natural forces. Sandstorms that engulf Northern Europe in its orange hue. An earthquake in the Philippines. Significant loss of life.

A fever that has led to the shut-down of a whole region of China. Dangers of economic collapse as the economy stops supply of products for the western markets. In Bangladesh the worst rainfall in 30 years brings flood, death and misery to millions of people settled along the Ganges basin.

An area of ice the size of Scotland falls into the ocean as the Arctic circle warms up. The threat of a one metre rise in sea level puts low lying environments in peril. The Dutch call on the European Union to consider a massive investment in flood protection.

'Bugger me, random events? Is it worth getting up for? Having a wash even? Perhaps it's the radiation in those huge masts they've built. 5G has a lot to answer for. Those shots, pulses of electricity, immense wireless speeds that are happening continuously. Can't be good for our health, or the health of the planet.

Perhaps I should throw something on social media. Get people's heart rate going a bit.

But I'll have to do a bit of research. Can't get away with it all just being in my head. Got to show a shred of validity. If I'm to attain viral ambitions!

Hmmmm, cash flow not so good. There's money in being an armchair social influencer, but I'm not there yet. So the Philippines is out, as is Bangladesh and China. And you can forget the Arctic!

Yeh, can probably stretch to a short trip to the Sahara.

He does a flight price scan.

Ah, OK. Bristol to Marrakesh, £167 return by Pennyflights. Book it man, book it.

He does a search for short breaks into the sahara.

So, Rana Tours. 3 day Sahara break. Ride camels. See the ancient city of Ouarzazate, walk through the Todgha Gorge. Sleep in a Bedouin tent in the Sahara. 90 euro. Not really. Yet. Negotiable, I'm sure. But only if I can get free wi-fi.

Right. Booked. Suppose I'm going to have to get dressed to do this. Do I need to wash my jeans as well? Nah, bugger that.' He raises his head. 'Yo Rick, thought I couldn't organise a piss up in a brewery?   Well, I'm off on the road to Marrakesh, screw you mate.'

He hears a voice in his head saying *Good choice, you're going to revel in this one.*

…..……………………………………..

5   Seville, Spain….

A MODEL reads the Spanish edition of Vogue and also flicks through her Instagram feed. She sips at a lemon drink. She glances over, gives her boyfriend the eye and speaks

'Jose, does my bum look big in this outfit? I'd like to take it on holiday but not sure that it's suitable. What do you think?

She takes a positive reaction even though Jose merely shakes his head.

How much luggage are you taking Jose? I was thinking like 2 suitcases. I know the luggage allowance is only 15kg but I've been waiting months for this break. You know that. You know that Anna is taking 23 kg?

Yes, I know, she's flying with Iberian and we're flying bog standard Cheapaschips. Look, it's 65 euro for the extra baggage and I'm not taking less clothes to Anna. Don't know why she has to take so much anyway. With that body she could get away with wearing her scruffs for 2 weeks and the guys would still have their tongues out. Bitch. And how come we're slumming it with Cheapaschips?

All her fault anyway. Telling us she's met this like corporate marketing guy in Casablanca and she's going out to visit him and wouldn't it be nice if we like strung along and maybe visited some of the sights….and she knew I wouldn't say NO! And you certainly jumped at the idea.

She takes her breath and goes back to the magazine.

Wonder how I could get on the Vogel modelling listings? I bet half of them slept with the talent scouts. Bitches.

Jose, when we get back I'm going to send some e-mails and my CV to Vogel, see if I can get my butt on the front cover. I can match any of these sleeze chicks. Oh, look at her, all tits and teeth, well actually they are nice tits, actually really nice tits.

Jose, are my tits OK?

She doesn't wait for a response.

So, we're booked in to the Fairmount Royal Palm, Marrakesh. That's like 14 in the top 20 hotels on Trip Watch. Why didn't you book something better? Anna is staying at the 4 Seasons in

Casablanca which is a 5 star and number 4 on the ratings, and she got an upgrade with complimentary massage. Call this a holiday of a lifetime Jose? You suck.'

....

6   Stuttgart, Germany.....

An ARCHITECT is reading from a manual. She makes some notes on a piece of paper. Some complex building calculation she is puzzling with. She puts the manual down and turns her attention to her cell phone and starts to type.

Sven

Have you heard the awful news? There has been some strange earth movements in Agadir, Morocco. Just outside the city. It happened yesterday evening. Apparently there is a loss of life among several workers who were in an office block where it happened. There has been an initial inspection and the area safety inspector has made comments suggesting that the building should have withstood the movements, and is stating publicly that there were structural issues to be investigated. As the design architect I have to go out there soon as I can get an available flight. The firm have given me full backing and I know in my heart that the design of that building was structurally sound.

I know how hard this is for you. I know I should be here for you on your return. I miss you dearly and hope you are coping OK out there in Bangladesh. I imagine the conditions in that refugee camp are terrible .... you are such a brave man, my liebe. But when I get back we can be together again and have that break in the Swiss mountains we have talked about.

Stay safe. Katrin

She turns back to her paper

'Architectural and design flaws? Pah. Mensche! No way did I compromise on safety. 4 years studying, 2 years post graduate and 3 more years in building design and they say it was a design fault. More like Moroccan building standards and Moroccan materials. I'm not going to be the fall guy for this one.

Nun ja, I must go. Let's see if Flughappy can fly me there via Stuttgart.'

She shifts to her mobile phone

…………………………………………..

7   Bogota, Colombia……and Madrid International Airport

A regional POLITICIAN is typing a message on Chatupp. Accused of, among other things embezzlement….and adultery. He's big on the importance of marriage. Hypocrite, many lovers, wife won't speak to him. Also evidence of him visiting prostitutes, possibly living off earnings. Left Bogota just as the newspaper Bogota Post was about to dish the dirt.

An announcement comes over the airport communications….. This is Madrid International Airport. Passengers on AirPacific flight CP194 from Bogota to Bangkok please go to AirPacific customer service desk where a member of staff will advise you of your onward journey.

The politician sends a message on his feed

#stuck in Spain.......so my flight to Bangkok suddenly cancelled due to virus outbreak in China and SE Asia#

He tries to make a phone call to Morocco but can only leave a message....

'Bro, can you pick up? I'm grounded at Madrid International due to flight being cancelled. It's this fever thing. I've got to leave Spain before the shit hits the fan about a few personal issues back home. I think the news won't filter through to Morocco so need a few days with you to let the heat die down and work out a strategy. I'll explain when I see you.

My flight leaves in 3 hours, arriving Marrakesh at 18.35 local time. Can you meet me at the airport? I'll not be in your hair for long, I just need a bit of time to sort out what to do next.

Can you pick up?

He puts the phone down and speaks to himself.

I'll have to phone ThaiCupid. They need to know I'm not going to get there. 3,000 dollars down the river all because of an over hyped up cold. Hopefully the Colombian papers don't feature out in Bangkok. They'll maintain confidentiality. Damage limitation. Now.'

CHAPTER 9

CHIPS

A quiet sandy breeze flows through the dense warren of paths and tunnels, battlements and towers of the tired old structure one might call a castle. The King sits, twiddling his thumbs pondering why he had to shout out so loudly after the skeletal Cassim urged him to use his powers to summon earthly beings. He calls on Cassim to arise from his stupor.

'Vizier, it has been enough time. I have become impatient. I summoned the seven souls from mortal earth and…..nothing. Tell me you are not setting me up as the fool that you already are.'

Cassim rattles his chains in a pretence at being scared. He has been around this place and this being too long to worry much about consequences. Let's face it, when you're dead there's not much worse that can happen. 'Sire, the wheels of fate are already turning. They are turning through the medium of the silcon chip, the sand of time that you follow and admire so much. The seven are, as I speak receiving instruction concerning their travel to the Sahara. But it is important for the seven to travel and meet without suspicion. So you'll have to be patient you old fool. The time will come.'

The King overlooks the blatant cheek of Cassim. He is pleased that events are on the turn. He speaks. 'Cassim, amuse me, tell me how this silicon chip works for I do not comprehend its power. And what was all that about some Cyclops? I seem to remember that was something from about three thousand years ago.'

'Sire, the chip is everywhere. It has transformed the very nature of how mortals behave. Not only does it turn the wheels of industry, and indeed, turns them very efficiently with nothing like the amount of materials that were needed in previous times, it allows communication to travel globally between people. Cyclops is the corpoation that is amassing more control over it, even to providing everyday shopping needs.'

'Yes, but does its power equal that of the wheel, or glass... another one of the great inventions of sand?'

'Sire, the remarkable nature of the silicon chip is the very dependency on it for many things. And the fact that it has usurped knowledge. Now everyone is a seer, by the all embracing power of Goggle, but, although knowledge is to be found everywhere, it has been devalued as a consequence, and mortals now struggle with knowledge that is deliberately falsified for political and economic gain.

But here's the rub. The silicon chip is flawed. Not of itself, but by man. You see, man is able to make a virus from the chip that corrupts the very being of its worth. Not a virus that the queen has been unleashing for millenia, no, not a biological virus, but a delibareate creation that causes misery and havoc on a massive scale. And then it takes another chip to rid the system of its disease.'

The King considers this last comment. 'Power corrupts and he who controls the manufacture of news corrupts absolutely. I'm looking forward to meeting the seven, but I wonder what they will make of it all.'

CHAPTER 10

SIGHTS & SPICES

Flying into Marrakesh was a relatively starightforward event. Each of the seven had a flight time of no more than 4 hours, if you excused the layovers at Charles de Gaulle and Madrid. Although they all travelled on different flights at different times, passport control and customs were simple and uncomplicated. Not even a temperature check. Baggage came out reasonably quickly and within 40 minutes of landing they had each, on different days, found a way into the city, a journey of approximately 20 minutes by taxi.

Over the next few days the seven explored Marrakesh and the area around in their own individual ways. And each of them experienced the Moroccan approach to life and tourism quite uniquely.

For Alain, he soon discovered that if you wanted to get around you either had to book a coach in advance or use the taxis. Local buses were a nightmare for him. He decided that a trip to Agadir was a good idea until he found out that the only coach going there was at 9am the following morning and it was a three hour drive. He hadn't booked ahead and realised that if he didn't sort out a room he'd be there the night without accommodation. He turned his attention to Essouira, found that a coach was leaving the next day at the respectable time of 11.30 in the morning and got two nights accommodation booked in the square, near the parapets of the ancient castle.

That evening Alain went out to eat at a reasonably priced local restaurant. As it was Friday it was cous cous night so he ordered a lamb and chicken combined, a bottle of water and finished off with an ice cream pancake. He got back to his room and for the rest of the night made over a dozen visits to the john. 'Crap, a dodgy meal, bollocks, bollocks. Cous cous, bloody tagine, whatever.' For the next two days he stayed in, drank boiled water that one of the staff brought to his room and ate only toasted bread at breakfast.

…………………………………………………..

Gabriella and Jose wandered around the fountain at Place 16 Novembre. They'd had their second coffee and were bored. Gabriella had met up with Anna earlier and was a little uneasy about the way Jose and Anna were behaving. She let it go but it kept coming back to her. As they were passing a souvenir shop Gabriella stopped to look at some crystals and local jewellery. While in the shop the guy asked them if they had been to the waterfalls. A must see while in Marrakesh apparently. 'The Ouzoud waterfalls, my friends, very beautiful. And monkeys too. You can take boat and go under the waterfalls, very big fun. I can get you good price, my brother, he has tour agency. Only 3 hours by air conditioned coach. And for you sweet madam, I give you extra discount because you have beautiful hair.' They asked for a price, got it further reduced by a third and said OK. Tomorrow was a day at the Ouzoud waterfalls.

…………………………………………………..

The train to Casablanca left 15 minutes later than it should have done. Mitch looked at his watch and mumbled something about timetabling and how Mussolini wouldn't have put up with it. A day trip to Casablanca. Only one reason to go thought Mitch: to visit Rick's Cafe. He'd seen the movie and although no huge fan of Bogart and Bacall he loved the atmosphere and the tension. The train ride was quite a slow one, certainly not rapid and apart from a few little tensions among two passengers went well. Mitch climbed down from the train at Casablanca station and faced the onslaught of taxi drivers wanting to take him to the city centre. He avoided them for a while, preferring to walk a little and get his bearings. He then found he had to navigate his way past several beggars who were asking for money with outstretched hands. He coldly gave them a stare and walked by, putting his hand up as if to say don't bother me, I'm too important for backshish.

Forty minutes later he'd given up looking for the Ancienne Medina, the site of Rick's Cafe and decided to humble himself and ask. 'Scuse moi, ou et le cafe Rick sil vouz plait', he reeled off in a French sounding accent.   'Oh, you want Rick's Cafe, famous cafe sir. Hey, I take you there in a while after I show you my brother carpet shop. Best prices, cheap as chips.' Mitch gave a big sigh and moved on. He asked the question again, this time to someone who didn't look like he had a brother and a carpet shop. '2 streets down messeur, to the left. Oh, you know ees no original, Hollywood reality, built in studio.' Rick found the cafe and couldn't believe his eyes. Of all the gin joints indeed. Whatever had been there, well it had been transformed into a classy restaurant and a need to book 24 hours in advance. Today, as luck would not have it, all tables were fully booked. It was indeed a stunning place and at least he got to have a look at it and take a cheeky gin martini before being asked politely to leave, as the table he was sitting in was about to to be taken by a family of four.

Well that was enough of Casablanca. Same shit, just a different city. He found his way back to the rail station and boarded the 16.45 to Marrakesh, a four hour journey. One hour in the conductor came around to check tickets. 'Sir, your ticket is only one way, not return.' Mitch looked up and his face started to redden. He could feel the fury. 'But I asked and paid for a return - Marrakesh to Casablanca, day return is what I said.' 'Monsieur, this is single ticket, you must pay difference, it will be 90 dirhams, or 10 euros. Cash only.' Mitch made it very clear that he was not paying again for a ticket he had paid for. The conductor asked to see his passport and noted the number. Mitch demanded to know why he needed this information. 'I must phone my supervisor so that when you arrive Marrakesh he speak you. No pay, you see the police.' And with that Mitch boiled over and shouted. 'Allright, allright, here's your money.' And then he turned his attention to the other passengers. 'And thank you all for being a lovely audience.'

….……………………………………………………

It was Friday afternoon around 2pm when Padre Alfonso decided to leave his room and take a walk along the main boulevard in the city, near the fountain and roundabout. A popular spot with tourists, plenty of coffee shops and a newly constructed shopping medina. Very expensive clothes, jewellery and leather goods. Nothing like the popular square 2 miles away. Chaotic, vibrant and full of character.

It was getting hot as the afternoon kicked in, but for mid March not unpleasant. Alfonso decided he would get a taxi to take him to the Djemma El Fna square and try and unwind a little in the cheaper area of the city. The tourists were out and so were the traders, street hustlers and a variety of entertainers all looking to lighten the purse with snake charming, acrobatics, dodgy loud piped music and numerous opportunities to have a photograph with a monkey perched on the shoulder. He had noticed one western tourist having an altercation with a local over a disputed photograph he had apparently taken of a troupe of musicians. The tourist was shouting very loudly that although he might have his mobile phone out, it didn't necessarily mean he was taking shots.

Alfonso moved on and had a drink of bottled water, avoiding many offers to eat at a very good price in some of the street food stalls. It didn't really impress him and he was wondering whether there was a way to pass some time out of the city altogether.

Without realising it he had found himself next to the holy mosque situated just off the square. Dozens of men were leaving following afternoon prayer. He became very uneasy as men dressed in white long shirts and caps brushed into him. And a few had noticed his rosary and uttered some disparaging comments among their own kind. In an instant several people had gathered and began shouting at him. It took a police officer who happened to be nearby to break things up and he politely spoke to the padre 'maybe best if you move along, you are drawing attention to yourself.' Padre Alfonso eyed the police officer, turned on his heels and walked away. 'Heathen.'

And then the voice entered his head again.

…………………………………………………………..

Gabriella, Jose and Anna boarded the minibus at 7.30 am and headed off on the three hour journey to the Ouzoud falls. Gabriella hadn't really fully awoken and the fact that Jose and Anna were speaking quite playfully didn't figure in her head. She decided to use the three hours for a little shut eye and plugged in her earphones and listened to Katy Perry's greatest hits. She was still angry with Anna, after all this time, for getting the two of them involved in her career opportunities out in North West Africa. Why couldn't she just work in Spain. And why didn't that jerk Ernesto get in touch: Gabriella was slow to forgive and even slower to forget.

They arrived at the falls and walked the short distance from the coach stop to the top of the waterfall. It was a stunning site and the opportunity for as many selfies as possible kicked in. She shouted for Jose to take some photos of them BOTH. Anna could sort out her own photo gallery. Jose took a few shots without showing much interest. They walked down to the base of the waterfalls and boarded a flat bottomed boat to float over to where the falls hit the bottom. Everyone got wet and everyone, apart from Gabriella found it massive fun. 'My hair is soaked, look at me. I look like a drowned rat' Jose responded. 'That just about sums you up.' 'What's that supposed to mean?' To which Jose bit his lip and said 'Gabriella, I wasn't going to say anything until we got home, I've had enough. It's over. It's all about you, you never say thank you, you never compliment. We're done.' And Gabriella then noticed the looks that he and Anna were giving each other. 'You absolute bitch.'

…..

Katrin returned from Agadir after three days of intense scrutiny over the language and content of the original design drawings. Of course everything had to be translated into two languages, French and Arabic so the matter was time consuming and it was so important that nothing was lost in translation, or mis-interpreted. From her company point of view, it was all about the materials, not the design. So when Katrin flatly refused to accept any liability for the collapse, she insisted that only a full inquiry into the methods of construction and materials used would unearth who if anyone was to blame. The city mayor and the chief of police agreed that nobody should be blamed at such an early stage and suggested that some local civil engineers be brought in to investigate.

Katrin shook her head. 'My company will have to agree who will conduct this investigation, so you will need to give me their names and their portfolios so I can consult with my superiors. Here's my email adress and contact details. I'll be in Marrakesh for a few days. Talk about a root and branch investigation - it will be roots, branch and all the leaves my friend.' It was at this point she decided to bring forward her journey back to Marrakesh and find three days to soul search.

…..…..

Phil had found himself in the souk near Djemma El Fna. He had already got the backs up of some street entertainers following an incident where money was demanded from him for apparently taking photos off his mobile phone. 'I don't use my mobile for photos, I've got a bloody £300 camera for that' he protested to the brightly coloured musician wearing a large Mexican style hat. 'So, bugger off, and by the way the hat is so out of place.'

He continued wandering around and was soon stopped by one of the local 'tour guides' who was really keen on showing Phil the sights and the crafts of the souk. 'Come with me, where you from…. England, ah OK, Manchester United, Paul Pogba, very good player, French oui. I show you very special shops with ceramics, copper and marble pieces. Very nice and good price for you. The owner, he speaks only Berber, from the Sahara. He uses special skills.'

Phil shrugged his shoulders and followed. The 'guide' walked him through the narrow alleyways past traders and craftsmen beating copper dishes, dusting off carpets and clothing, re positioning souvenirs moved by tourists and trying to get him to buy spices from huge mounds of red, yellow and brown powders. Phil wasn't massively impressed and resignedly followed further into the market. They arrived at a shop where the owner greeted them with a mint tea. After ten minutes of hard selling tactics the owner had decided that Phil wasn't going to buy anything and waved his hand and shooed him away. The 'guide' moved in and asked Phil if he wanted to see another shop. Negative. Then it was a request for some consideration, some backshish. Phil's response was terse and to the point 'I never said I would pay you to walk me around the stalls. You never said you wanted payment when we set off. I've seen so much of this stuff, all the same and I'll bet most of it is imported from China. Thank you, but no thank you.' The guide cursed him very loudly and tried to grab his camera, but Phil pushed him away and marched off, and soon reaslised that he was completely lost in the warren that was the Marrakesh souk. It took nearly an hour and several botched up attempts back and to before he found the main entrance and made a hasty B line for a western style fast food take away.

…………………………………………………………

Despite several knocks and ringing on the doorbell there was no answer. He looked through the window and couldn't see any activity. A couple of mangy cats were sizing up to each other nearby and a neighbour was eyeing Pablo Mendes rather suspiciously. 'Have you seen the guy who lives here, Juan Sebastian, I'm his brother?' 'He's away, I think for a week. Business trip I think he said.'

'Mierda. Now what do I do. I'll have to book in at some rank hotel.' Pablo Mendes picked up his luggage and walked out in the hope of flagging a taxi. After a twenty minute ride he went to the reception at the Sofitel Spa Hotel and booked in for five days. He dumped his belongings in his room, went back downstairs and asked where the nearest shop selling foreign newspapers was…. oh, and a hamam. He needed to unwind.

He was relieved to see that nothing of any interest had been printed about events in Bogota and made his way to the nearby hamam where he would plan his next move.

'30 Dirham for the bathe, 15 Dirham for the towel, 10 Dirham for the slippers. You want massage too? OK, 20 Dirham for massage…. 75 Dirham.' The man behind the desk passed him a large white towel and wooden slippers and ushered over a bearded man carrying a sponge and cotton rag.

Pablo Mendes felt the weight of his recent stresses slowly unwind as the bearded masseur laid pressure on his back and legs. Pablo Mendes was wondering how long he would have to endure

North West Africa before he could resume his ambitions in Thailand. Perhaps this short break away might help clear his mind.

CHAPTER 11

THE ROAD FROM MARRAKESH

A white coach bus arrives outside Rana Tours offices in Marrakesh near the Djemm El Fana square and parks up alongside a shop where the noise of metal being hammered rings in the ear. A cigarette seller tries to negotiate the price of 20 fake Marlbro to a passing tourist. Another tourist is struggling to get some money out from an ATM.

The driver/tour guide opens up the rear door and waves to indicate he wants people to put their bags in the space. Then he ushers in the waiting tourists who settle in and unpack their snacks and water. Out come the mobile phones and in go the earphones.

He gets in the driver seat and enters his navigation details. Then takes a swig of bottled water and adjusts his seat.

'Okay guys, 7 of you on the tour – yes?' He looks behind him and counts out loud while pointing….1,2,3,4,5,6 and 7. 'You all like Marrakesh eh? Crazy city. City of dreams, city of joy, city of mystery. My name is Amir. I speak good English, aand French, a littel German.

Have you all got your paper receipts? Good. Remember for the meal and soft drinks you'll have to buy extra, also camel ride is not included. If you want to book – you can tell me, when we arrive at the camp site. Really beautiful, okay? We're now driving to the desert plain – please check the time, my friends – different zone, yes? I don't want you get lost and start looking for you. Air conditioning unfortunately no working so if it get too hot just shout I open window. You all have brought enough water? If not, I have cooled water here in the front, you can buy with cash or credit card. American Express very welcome. If you use internet, please no movie or naked. Seat belts, it's up to you. Not my problem. Okay? Jallah, off we go. We'll have a toilet stop in about 2 hours and you can drink coffee.'

The coach drives through the busy streets avoiding the occasional donkey and cart and drifting pedestrians carrying goods to market. Outside of the city the seven are heading out to the foothills of the Atlas mountains. It's a pleasantly hot day, around 33 degrees but inside the coach it's sticky and smells of sweat. Now aboard the coach the seven strangers are setting out on a short trip to the Saharan desert for a 3 day trek– they are still unknown to each other.

The coach bus has 8 rows of seats.

1 row is THE DRIVER, wears sunglasses and sucks on a lollypop.He has a loose file next to him with the details of his clients, but not much more detail than who paid and by what method. Not even their phone numbers and contact details in case of emergency. But then, this is Morocco.

2 row is THE MODEL, drinking a lot of water and making selfies. She's wearing a white top and denim shorts and smiles a lot.

3 row is THE CHEF, eating candy, nachos and marshmallows. He takes up most of the two seats and notices the model in front of him. He thinks of things with sexual desire.

4 row is THE BLOGGER, making pictures of the landscape, expensive camera gear, He mutters quite a lot and scribbles some notes in an A4 school workbook.

5 row is THE ARCHITECT, working and making notes, listening to some rock music on her Iphone and red as a lobster.

6 row is THE POLITICIAN, reading a crime novel, wearing a panama hat and swiping through photos he keeps in his phone gallery.

7 row is THE BUSINESSMAN, sweating a lot, pushing all levers, knobs and stuff he can find, checking his watch.

8 row is THE PADRE, wearing his full gown and rotating a metal rosary in his hands. He is the only person to wear a face mask.

The businessman sits near the rear of the bus and dries his neck with a sweat cloth. He takes a drink of water. He plays around with the curtains and the seat belt and checks his watch, again. Looking ahead of him and to the side he starts off with a very forward…

'So how much did you guys pay for this trip? I'm telling ya those A-rabs, they know how to make a buck – that's what they know. Trying to rip you off for everything. I had all the meals included – they told me before - and I will tell them! Negotiated hard, I got them down by half. I'm Mitch by the way. USA, Boston. Anyone from Germany? I can speak fluent German too.'

The chef groans and puts another handful of nachos in his mouth. He is the first to respond to Mitch.

'Mon dieu, most of the food here is pah, why would you even eat-a that – it's just bland. To be honest, I don't know why they're saying the food here is good …' He looks to the model posting a photo of herself in a bikini on her cell phone.

The chef continues '… this whole country is just a backpacker-scam. Eat. Pray. Love putain fus de la merde, mange pas de cien – it just looks good on your selfies, all fake.'

The model notices him eyeing on her picture feed and shuts her phone off. She looks back and smiles.

'Hi, Mitch I'm Gabriella, from Spain. Sorry I don't speak German but my English is pretty good. I'm from Seville, you know it? Famous city, UNESCO heritage and all that.

As for food, well, I had this super cool tagine with sea salt flakes and lemongrass yesterday and they served it on this rooftop – it had like these colourful umbrellas and OMG it was so delicious! But it's not like on the apps, it's like the locals go there and only a few people know it.'

She sips some water from her bottle and checks her mobile phone, trying to keep it away from the gaze of the chef. The chef adjusts his posture uneasily and looks out of the window. He wades in 'I bet-a you paid-a more than you would in Europe, ah? What is it? Come-ca - Legumes avec chicken stew? Beaucoup de trolles? No?'

He stuffs a nacho in his face and turns back to face the blogger. 'And your name is?'

The blogger lifts his head away from the book he's been scribbling in and looks at the chef. 'I'm Phil, from Bristol in England and you, I'm guessing you're French by your accent?' 'Je suis Alain, chef, from Lyons in France.'

The mountains in the background are fading away. And there is dust blowing over the rocky plain. Phil is preparing his camera to take some shots of the landscape. He puts down his note book and starts to type a few notes into his tablet.

Rick, my god, this place is like no other place, like we're on Mars. This whole trip is just getting surreal – have you heard of this earthquake that happened here in Morocco? Well buddy, it happened back in the '60's. And now they also have this pandemic spreading like wild fire. Not seen anyone local wearing masks though. At least the rural areas here are not yet affected.

Nature is still the escape. I' ll send on a few pics so you can look at this magnificent landscape! You should have come along bud. Missed opportuntity to align yourself with some weird shit!

The driver spots his interest in his rear view mirror… 'Yes take pictures- very beautiful landscape. Maybe you see tree with goat. Right now is still calm – sometimes have big storms here. Everybody comfortable? Anyone from Australia? Last week we had 3 Australian tourists on tour. They all went down with illness, maybe mosquito, maybe Chinese flu. But, hey, no worry I am fine. See, no sweat, no cough hahaha.'

The architect picks up on the driver's comments about storms as she is making notes and working/reading. She drops her sunglasses onto the tip of her nose and looks out.
'You mean sandstorms? The famous Saharan glow. Orange in pigmentation, because a lot of iron deposits. That's why their Rebar starts rusting without rain. That's why the earthquake hit them so strong back in the 1960's. It's materials–infrastructure.' She turns to the politician behind her and speaks quietly.
'Poor workmanship and, they also have no hospitals standards, like we do. Luckily we in my country have still the lowest mortality rate in this virus pandemic. Oh, by the way I'm Katrin, from Germany, Stuttgart to be precise.'

The businessman chips in. 'Hah, wait until this place gets connected to the pipeline from the Casablanca oil field. Then you have this wasteland here colonized in a year. Will put huge money into their pockets. And cut off those Arabs – all Chinese money anyway. Look at Dubai – was a desert twenty years ago – now has the best doctors and medical schools in the world. Top standard – all built by the Arabs with their oil money. Biggest supplies are buried under sand. Who would've guessed that the deserts will one day be the richest places.'

The architect is double crossing and underlining something in her book but keeps her attention on the conversation. 'It is everywhere the same. If you want to connect to the people – you just don't go where tourism is. And Morocco has such beautiful culture and cities. I was here back in 2019, big project in Agadir. Office block construction. Oh I love this place. Unique. Berber folk. It is such a shame – that they cannot keep up to their old craftsmanship. Sure everything is collapsing.'

The driver picks up a little speed on the straight and overtakes a lorry which is leaning precariously to the left. They both toot a signal and flash their lights. Either side of the road the buildings start to decrease in number and there is a noticeable change in the environment. Definitely more sand and less traffic. The company of seven have started their introductions and are now chatting a little more easily. However, secrets remain secrets and the conversation is very much on the journey details and little else. The padre sits and watches but is reserved over any conversation. It's hotting up now and the driver winds down the window to allow for the 'air condtioning' to take effect.

The politician leans over and fixes his gaze on Katrin. 'So you're German! I met a few Germans back in my home country, Colombia, you know, South America? Si, Very nice peoples, very charming. They were on a business trip. My name is Pablo.' He realises that he shouldn't give too much away, just in case he's appeared in the press, so he reigns himself in. 'Pablo….Estevez, I ….uhhh….own a small taxi company in Medellin. Nice to meet you Katrin. You are right about this country, young lady. Look at this place, I mean, let's not call it third world but...everything is collapsing, we're in the eye of the storm, even here. I mean I've hardly seen a face mask on anyone but it's coming. Just before we left I received the latest updates for my own country – wealthy community … but this pandemic – we had to close everything. I will not be able to return.

Three weeks shutdown – for safety. Imagine that – locked out from your own district. All I can do is wait and pass time, no work.'

Mitch pipes in, a little too loudly for the space they occupy. 'Phew, don't ask me – I was supposed to transit for a very important meeting – I'm talking close to a billion dollars – and they cancelled, because the border shut – and now second best thing: I'm on a shitty tourist bus trip and have wait this one out – no offence guys …'

Gabriella puts down her mobile phone and looks in the drivers mirror to speak to the others behind. 'OMG, that sounds terrible. So do you like, have family back home Pablo? You must be worried. And hey, Mitch, if you don't mind me asking, but why did you come on the trip, if you don't like it?'

'Hey guys, I was just saying, nothing personal. Why did I come on this trek? Hah, because they're closing the hotels - no more bookings. No nothing – I put it in cash. On the desk. No chance, because of the virus. Even cash money they didn't accept - that's how bad it is. This desert camp trip was the only accommodation next to sleeping on the airport. Plus free internet connection. I got lucky because our guide was in the lobby. Flight out in four days, when we return from the Sahara. By the way, have any of you got any news?'

Gabriella shifts uneasily and plays with her manicured fingernails, fidgeting and a little nervous. 'My piece of pooh ex-boyfriend got pulled over, when he tried to cross border back to Spain. Now he's in quarantine and probably faces jail time, together with this bitch he ran off with – serves him right. Cheating scum. I've got nothing outside – and I will stay this over in Morocco.' She sighs and forces a smile. 'Have a long vacation - right guys, best we can do!'

Katrin is quizzical. 'Are you staying in a Riad, Gabriella?' 'Oh my god, no, but they're so beautiful I like saw it on pictures of a friend of mine – she stayed here last year. Amazing. I love to go there – I'm thinking of adding a couple of days just for that. I'm in the Fairmount hotel right now, because they took a deposit for our, umm my return – and yeah it's top class, actually it's like the best ranked on travel advisor, but it's so distanced of the people. Yeah, so …'

The coach party pass on a few comments to each other about the quality of their accommodation, ranging from bearable to quite comfortble. The business of breakfast, Moroccan style is aired and the chef makes a passing comment about the way the Moroccans cook omelettes. Mitch talks over everyone, loudly. 'Just wait until they cancel the tourist flights from Europe, because of this flu thing. If you ask me it's just a hoax anyway, yeah maybe one or two with existing preconditions will get it, but people go crazy. Prices will plummet – give it two weeks and you can have top class hotels for the price of two stars. But I'll be back over the pond , business is still crazy.'

For the first time since the party got talking, the padre chips in on the conversation.
'Signore, I wouldn't take this illness so lightly – many, many people are suffering right now. And this is not just a hoax. The whole world is suffering. Virus, hunger, war. Maybe if we wouldn't be so fixed on prices, we could see what really happens.' He shuffles his rosary in his hands and resumes a stare through the coach window.

Members of the group look at Padre Alfonso; they are unable to find words in reply. Apart from Mitch. Mitch cannot resist an opportunity to say something. 'Preacher man, believe me, it's always the markets and never the people. Why else would they let us spend our money here, while half the world is under lockdown? Because of money!

Alright read your newspapers and all their crying is over this little flu, but you know what's the real headline? The oil price. Always has been - they just don't call it that way. They call it Iraq war, they call it terrorism, they call it migration crisis. Nope, it's oil. And boy, I can see this A-rab Argan oil price go through the roof. Shouldn't tell you this but it's got great additive properties to silicon.'

Mendes looks to the row below and fixes a gaze on Mitch. He's clearly agitated and can't stop himself 'Oh you Americans, if anyone should know it's your government with your wars. Your presidents comes down like locusts and take down the economies to keep other countries poor. Just imperialists, no different to the Ruskies.'

There's a call for a little calm in the coach and Katrin suggests maybe a change of conversation. Mitch is having none of it. 'Hey, speak to the preacher, pal. I know, but if it weren't for us you would still be sucking on the commies tits, besides we're not sitting on it. The Saudis are, and the A-rabs know how to make their dollar.' He gets a call on his cell phone and looks at the number frowning. He doesn't recognize it and shakes his head in puzzlement. 'Hello? Oh, goddamn voicemail.'

Gabriella now tries to send a few words of appeasement. 'O my god. You guys, always with the politic and the war, also I read that the Moroccans are like Berbers not Arabs and that is just racist and that is not cool. It's lame — and we're here for vacation and enjoy.'

Phil picks up his head out of his tablet and joins in. 'Actually it's the Saudis and China. They have this secret trade deal — you can look this up online and they know that peak oil has already happened and now want to get the gold standard back, and for that they have to reduce the population density — so what better way than to invent a killer illness. They even found the lab in

China, where they made it and the earthquakes: they tested this in South America – in the 70s - it's all online - they have sub-terrain nukes go off and the radiation destroys man made structures. Like the sand in the concrete if it hits the right wave length - they can do that. It's all on my blog.'

The conversation has now got just about everyone throwing in comments for good measure. The atmosphere is fairly relaxed despite the obvious political differences. The driver looks back to see what's happening, takes a swig of water and tosses a few peanuts in his mouth. Only the padre resists getting involved. It's now Katrin's turn. 'It has nothing to do with the earthquake. They used Sahara sand for building, but Sahara sand, the molecule is very round. Pebbles from wind erosion, but you need spiky crystal to make good concrete. That is why they had all this buildings going down. If you know what you are doing, you can build earthquake resistant. No problem.'

Mendes dismisses the gesture. 'All builders and constructers are corrupt, they use plywood for skyscrapers, if they can make money. Trust me, I've had to deal with crooks like these in my country all the time. Everybody is looking out for himself.'

Mitch again. 'Well, let's face it pal, if you're from Colombia; crime and racketeering goes with the territory, am I right?' Mendes feels his face go red.

The padre is still staring out of the window, his head heavy in thought.' The bible says it: the house built on sand: to those corrupt the lord had their temples shattered. It is all of man's own doing.' .

Gabriella was having second thoughts about the wisdom of this trip 'OMG, guys - you really should get off all those negative thoughts – you know. Because beautiful souls are beautiful and this is just negative. Come on, we're on vacation, chill out a little.'

Mendes looks toward her and his eyes make a B line for her low lying T shirt top. Gabriella notices and looks away. 'She's right – let's leave the crappy world outside for a couple days. We're here far away from oil, and virus and all this. Let's all have a good time in the desert, drink and forget and … I really have to take a piss now.'

Gabriella turns to the driver. 'Hey Amir, like can we take toilet stop. I've been drinking so much water – when is the next …' She points out of the window and reaching for her phone. 'WHOA! Look a tornado! Oh shoot, anyone got a cable – my battery is really low…'

Phil looks up from his phone. He mutters to himself. 'That's not a tornado – that's a sand devil.' And a voice in his head speaks to him and says '*Yes, you're correct, they don't know much do they*?'

Amir turns his head to the rear of the bus. 'They call it a dervish. It brings good luck, hahaha.' He rights the minibus as it veers to the left of the road and continues driving straight into the path of the oncoming sand storm.

Mendes now comments. 'That is not just whirlwind – look at that wall of sand there, are you going to turn around or what. Jeez, not seen anything like this since I watched Lawrence of Arabia 20 years ago.'

Gabriella. 'OMG, I thought that was the mountains – that is like a mother of a cloud!'
Mitch blares out to Amir. 'A cloud? Holy mother of god, that's a major sandstorm! Are you sure we're safe here?'

Amir looks to the rear again and continues driving. He gestures with his hand and points outside. 'No problem, sandstorm is very common. Sand no problem, everything here is sand. If rain, then problem. You know, is like a flood.'

It suddenly gets very dark, like it is night. The sandstorm blocks the sun, as the coach drives right through it. Amir switches on the headlights, for what that is worth. The sand starts to fly in from the window. Katrin screams.

Amir responds. 'Don't worry. This is normal for sandstorm - we just close air-conditioning, like camel nose. No problem.'

Mitch ponders and says to the driver 'Hey A-mer, I thought you said the air conditioning was broken. Is this charabanc safe to drive Mr?'

Gabriella looks to Katrin and whispers. 'OMG. How can he even see the road – I can see nothing. This is so exciting.' She turns to Alain. 'Hey – sorry, what is your name – could you take a picture of me? My battery is like, so dead. OMG, my friends won't believe that.'

Alain takes hold of her cell phone and, trying to play it cool says 'Yeah, sure – no problem. Alain.' Gabriella poses and smiles while the sandstorm fully immerses the coach .

Mendes has become very uncomfortable with the experience and plays around with his money belt. He looks at his cell phone. He looks around to see what type of expression the others are showing. There is a mixture of awe, excitement and, in the case of Alfonso who is staring out, complete nonchalance. 'Shouldn't we stop and wait this one out? You're going to drive us off a cliff.'

Amir takes a swig of water as he continues the journey. He puts it down and looks in the rear view mirror. 'No cliff. The mountains are BEHIND us they are in the past, only desert AHEAD. That is the future. No problem - bus has good parking assistant - makes Beep before Bang. All good. Hahahhaha.'

Mitch is now concerned as well. He tries to use his cellphone but realises there is no signal. 'He's not going to stop – we already paid him, now his time is his money. If this storm is going to ruin the trip – I will make them give me my money back. It's always money with these A-rabs. Damn, I will make a fortune from my insurance on this one.'

Amir steps on the brakes and the coach comes to a sudden halt.
Phil, who has been typing a text message for his blog onto his tablet, looks up and asks, confusingly 'What's wrong why are we stopping?'

Mitch. 'What's wrong? We're in the middle of this sandstorm. This guide just came to his senses. Jeez, driving around is suicide and we should better get off the road too.'

Amir opens the door, gets out and shouts to the travellers. 'No road closed. Road end here. We had sandstorm - everywhere else is closed. All is closed. Is closed. We're here now. Safe yes. Good driver huh, you make a good report on social media for me Hahaha.'

For most of the drive Mitch was of the view that someone in the party needed to take some leadership in case something like this happened. After all you can never trust the A-rabs. So he decided, unilaterally, that he would assume that role. Mitch could see it was his time. He fixes his eyes on his watch. Then he turns to Amir 'What do you mean, we're here now? The camp is supposed to be a six hour drive from the mountains. And I suppose that whole thing about a camel ride in the sunset, that was a scam too?'

Gabriella spoke next. 'Sunset, OMG, guys even the sun is blocked. Is it already getting dark?'

As quick as it came the sandstorm vanishes into few dusty gusts. Twilight settles around them. The road ahead is completely non existent and appears to simply vanish into the sand. It's as if the road has been swallowed into a great sink hole and sand is pouring in.

Now Phil starts to panic. 'Wait. Huh? On my watch it's still two o'clock in the afternoon. Do you guys have any signal? What is goin on?'
Mitch turns to Phil and laughs, mockingly. 'Call that a watch? This is a watch. My daddy bought it for me for my 16th. Keeps time to the nano second.'

He proudly shows off his watch to anyone who is near. Alain tries to show disregard to Mitch's pig headidness and looks away. He continues the conversation from Phil. 'Ah huh. No my phone went dead also. Probably a scam as well. Bought this cheap card at the Souks. They send me some voicemail to sell some rubbish and then it went dead.'

Katrin picks up her phone, looks into it, smiles and then frowns. She puts it down again. 'Yeah, strange. I had the same thing happening, but whoever jammed my in-box only left a poem. Internet trolls. Hmm, it seems the sandstorm is abating.'

Amir opens up the doors. 'So, storm is gone. Okay, please take bags out of bus. Camp is there.'
Amir very rudely throws some luggage (only Gabriella and Mendes brought luggage) out of the van

and drives off. The group is a little speechless, but yet too confused to stop him. Soon the van vanishes in the settling dust of dawn.

Gabriella is the first to speak. 'That guide has some nerves! How rude! That will get him a one star rating. Look at my bag, that was a coture. Not fake.' She takes off her high heels and walks barefoot in the sand. 'There are some tents over there, let's hope they have better service.' She looks at Alain and pouts. 'Oh, honey – could you be a sweetie and help me with this bag?' Alain, of course helps her with the bag, while Mendes struggles over the sand to pull his suitcase.

Padre Alfonso looks up to the air and raises his hands, his rosary wrapped around securely. 'Lost in the desert. How fitting. We should take the shelter.'

The seven walk towards the tents – which are raised in nomad tradition – old materials and heavily weathered. The closer they get, the more abandoned the camp looks. However there is one big tent in the middle, with some light glowing inside. As they enter the tent it seems completely empty, with two entrances to the outside. A blackish, green dome. There is the faint smell of sweet tobacco smoke rising from a hookah and a large pot of hot water boiling on a gas ring. The walls of the tent comprise of brightly coloured hanging carpets.

Somebody shouts out. 'Hello? Is anybody here.' A faint laugh echoes through the tent, but maybe it was the wind. Mendes, who arrives last with his bag gets angry. For Mendes, any attempts at being the diplomatic tourist has passed. He tosses it down and shouts 'Puta madre, this chingo place is a ruin …' He's interrupted by Alain 'Like I said all scams. Great – and my phone is dead … now we are stuck here.'

Mendes continues 'No way, that's it. I'm going back. I'll stop the next car that passes here.' As he tries to exit the entrance they came from he suddenly appears from the other entrance. He tries again. Same result. He's completely perplexed.

Katrin raises a smile and comments. 'No getting away through the out door.'

Mitch looks around and tries to get everone's attention. 'Where in the name of holy moly are we?'

CHAPTER 12

FACING YOUR DEMONS

A vortex starts to build up inside the tent. Not exactly a whirlwind or a typhoon, but a movement that happens outside of the seven which they can see but are unable to influence. It's as if everything is on the move apart from the seven. Indeed if you were to witness this you would swear that the group are fixed in a point and everything is moving around them. The vortex subsides. The travellers now find themselves in a dark place. Not quite a tunnel, not quite a room and certainly not a cell. One could call it something similar to a large pressure cooker. It is not barricaded. There are two openings. There is no evidence of a bedouin camp in sight. Sand is everywhere.

Gabriella looks around, completely puzzled. 'Hey, like, have we been kidnapped by terrorists or something? I don't understand. One minute we're riding along at a steady 55km/hr and then we're in some sort of hole. I mean like kidnap victims get such huge press attention. That's what I need now, some press attention. Get my own back on bitch Anna. And Jose.'

Phil responds, diplomatically. 'Nah, don't think so. Not as far as I'm aware. No terrorists in Morocco. This is something else.' He turns away and starts to talk to himself 'this is all part of a bigger plan isn't it......' and the voice inside his head speaks back *'yes, you knew something was going to happen didn't you. You were warned, weren't you?'*

Mendes, still confused over the door that he left and then re-entered mutters to himself 'Silly bitch, kidnappers and ransom, huh the doors to this place aren't even locked.'

Mitch wants to show leadership but finds the whole thing way past his pay grade. 'Where's that freaking driver. I demand a refund. This wasn't in the spec. What in God's name is happening? Look, I work for Cyclops Inc. I know people. I make things happen.' Everyone laughs.

'My time is money. Can't hang around he.....what you all laughing at? Cyclops, yes major IT corporation, Jeez.'

Alfonso approaches Mitch and prods him on the shoulder. 'It is not wise to take our lord's name in vain, Signor.' Alain tramps around and kicks the sand. He squashes a sand beetle with his boot. He hasn't eaten for a whole 40 minutes. 'And where's my food. I had a load of food on that charabanc. Did anyone catch sight of MY food?'

A voice from beyond is heard, a form unseen to the seven: the Queen speaks....'Food for thought, indeed.'

Katrin. 'What, who was that?' The 6 respond....wasn't me. 'And where is our driver? Amir, wassisname.'

Phil. 'I think someone is watching us.' He walks to the side and starts to talk to himself. 'This is no random event. *I know, I told you something would happen.* Can these other travellers be trusted? *I'm not sure about the BUSINESSMAN. And the POLITICIAN is definitely dodgy.* Yeah, he's holding something back. Not one to trust.

I know.'

Padre Alfonso walks up and turns to Phil. 'My child, is something bothering you? Do you hear the voice too?'

Mitch checks his watch again. He checks his cell phone. He smooths back his hair. 'Look, preacher, nerds and creeps, we have to get out of here. I've got business to do. This is no longer a relaxing 3 day Sahara Trek. It's a freakin disaster.'

The Queen again. This time to Mitch: 'A plague on your Cyclops empire.'

Mitch. 'What? What the hell is going on here?'

Alain. 'The Yank is correct. Well at the very least let's get out of here. Look, two openings.'
Gabriella picks up her bag and fumbles for a cigarette. 'What time is it? I seem to have, like, lost all sense of time.' Her hand is trembling as she lights her H&B.

Phil looks at his mobile phone. He shouts out loudly. 'Hey. Listen. I've just received a voicemail. Listen....' He turns up the volume. '...you are not the masters of your fates. Make a decision. Stay, move up or down.'

Alain demands to know who sent it and what it means. Phil shrugs his shoulders.
'Says it's from the Moirens.'   'Moirens, what the hell is Moirens?' Alain shouts back.

The Knave commands a position somewhere in the place we'll call a tunnel, or chute, or cylinder and speaks freely
<<I'll give it a few more moves baby, you ain't seen nothing yet>>

The JESTER, also out of sight of the seven now speaks:

It has started. Watch how the axis of power shifts. The Queen has made a move. The Knave will respond. I'll keep you all in the loop for a while as it may get complicated...and dirty.

Katrin looks up and shakes her head. Her face is puzzled. 'Was that Amir, the driver? Sounded like him, well, a bit. Don't recall him speaking quite like that on the trip though. What's he doing back here. I don't see him anywhere. Do you know something....' she looks to the others. 'I have absolutely no idea what motivated me to come on this 3 day trip. And now I wish I had simply flown home.'

The others, apart from the padre nod and puzzle. 'I never heard anything. And, yeah, actually, come to think of it I can't work out why I came on this nightmare of a journey either.'

Padre Alfonso speaks very slowly and deliberately 'It was decreed.'

Phil walks away from the others and starts talking to himself. 'Those messages, the moirens, that's all greek stuff about the fates. *What's greek philosophy got to do with all this?* I dunno, am I the only one hearing voices? *You're the only one hearing me and that's what matters.* Who to trust? *I'm working on it.* I don't trust the cell phones. *Me neither.'*

The JESTER speaks

Ah, he talks to himself as well. I'm in good company. No, I didn't mean you, reader, weren't taking this in, I meant..... well if you've got this far you must be taking it in.....sorry to sidetrack.....but you see I do talk to myself quite a lot, got no-one to listen, not pleasant. Sorry.

Gabriella stubs out her cigarette and fumbles in her bag 'My cellphone is dead. Like nothing. Last thing to appear was a name test… what type of person are you? Choose a door to reveal your personality….it showed me three personalities, someone called Clotho, Lachesis and Atropos. Don't even know if I've pronounced the names right. Ooh, they all look a bit serious. Duhh, who are they?'

Katrin muses over the names 'Hmmm those names are from the three fates, a piece of music by Emerson Lake and Palmer in the 1970's.' Phil listens curiously.

Alain scoffs "Nametests, ha. The social media equivalent of mirror, mirror on the wall. They always come up with "aww nice" comments. Just what people like to read, self congratulatory, complete bollocks. Umm, mine's dead too".

Mitch is still pacing around looking for an outlet or a grand plan. 'I've had a sqwalk posted

  #Cyclops Corporation to be investigated for misuse of company funds#.'

He looks at the others. 'Fake news my friends, fake news. Shoot, now it's dead too.'

The Queen looks down on the group and finds time to smile. For a moment the void is filled with light, but then returns to a dusky grey. Katrin looks at her cellphone 'Ah, Sven has posted me a song lyric from Peter Gabriel. Love Peter Gabriel

I looked up at the tallest building
  Felt it falling down
  I could feel my balance shifting
  Everything was moving around
  These streets so fixed and solid
  Ah shimmering haze
  And everything that I relied on disappeared

Downside up
    Upside down
    Take my weight off the ground
    Falling deep in the sky
    Slipping into the unknown

It's from Downside Up, love it. But why that, and now. He doesn't usually send me song lyrics. Wait a minute, is this to do with that building in Agadir? It was not my fault. Oops, mine's lost the signal too.'

The Queen speaks down to the group. 'And those that build a house on sandy ground shall see it fall. Mortals, the order of things is changing. My sirens gather.'

Padre Alfonso is playing with his rosary and quietly chanting a hail mary to himself. He stops temporarliy and shouts out 'The voice, I hear the voice, taken from the book of Matthew. The piece questions the very foundation of our lives. And as for sirens, well that's more Greek rubbish. Brothers and sisters we are being challenged as to our faith.'
He makes a sign of the cross 'In nomini patri et fili et spirituo sancti.'

Everyone looks at him perplexed. 'We all heard it!'

Phil checks his mobile phone. 'Another voicemail....from, Anna(?) to, to Gabbie? She says she has left Casablanca without Jose. He's being held back. She's back in Madrid. She's so sorry and wants you to forgive her.' Gabriella simply tuts and sticks her nose in the air. 'As if.' The group look at each other, look around the bareness of the void. They feel powerless as to what to do next. Mendes breaks the silence.

'Are we going to do something?' He looks up. 'What are we doing here and why have I not heard a thing. Not from my secretary, my brother, the agency in Bangkok. Apparently not even anything in the press about me.'

The party look at him and Katrin speaks 'Why would there be anything in the press about you?'

The Knave speaks to himself. <<Something tells me that all is not well with the politician, no doubt the Queen will play him>>

The JESTER speaks

Methinks the Queen is making another move. Not strictly a legal one. Keep an eye on the politician.

Phil moves to the centre of the group and speaks excitedly. 'I've sussed it. These so called random occurrences. Viruses, earthquakes, famine, mass emigration, asylum chaos. It's NOT random. It's all linked. Look I told you in so many words as we were travelling here. I know, I'm a blogger, I write shite, but this is NOT random.

Right. What made us all decide to come on this tour? Chance? I'll hazard a guess that each of us was influenced in some way by technology. I got a so called Bookmyflight price reduction. Didn't know Bookmyflight even did price reductions.

It's to do with viruses. People infected, technology infected. Energy pulses. Why is it I can only receive information but cannot transmit? Are you all the same?'

Everyone nods, apart from the padre. 'I do not have a mobile phone.'

But Mendes is still agitated and annoyed at himself for almost blowing some semblance of cover after speaking about press coverage. 'So why are we here, English nerd? I was supposed to be in Bangkok, then the flight is cancelled, then I fly out to Marrakesh. Then I go on a 3 day safari. Where's the conspiracy behind that? And anyway, I'm still not picking up anything on my phone. Maybe I'd get a better reception somewhere outside of this black hole we're in?'

He walks off away from the group and after about ten yards can no longer be seen. The group call him to come back and stay safe in company. Alfonso shouts in his direction 'You are very disrespectful and have no right to speak with the man in this way...'

Alain chips in. 'Blogger, blagger bullshit. Basically, you're nuts. Just another of these conspiracy theorists. Seen them all. It's the Chinese, it's the water, it's technology, it's religion. It's all bollocks.'

Katrin walks up to Alain and gives him a face off. 'Can you just for one moment not use the word bollocks every time you open your big mouth?'

The Knave speaks. <<Time to make a move>>

Gabriella. 'OK guys, I've had enough of this place. I'm like going upside. Upside, hey, where did that dope word come from?'
Alfonso challenges her. 'And what about Anna? Will you forgive her. Cast aside your envy?'   'Are you serious? No way pa-dre. Hey, like that. No way pa-dre, kinda rhymes. Anyone coming with me?'
She moves away from the group.

Katrin rolls her eyes. 'Has anyone noticed the passage of the sun? It seems to be setting over in the east. I have a compass and it's shifting all over the place but the sun is definitely setting over in the east. Don't you see it. No, I guess not. Idiots.'

The Queen muses to herself. 'A move by the model to the upside would be a good move, in my opinion, provided she tames her envious streak. The architect is becoming aware, which is a good start, but her pride is getting in the way. As for this businessman, I think he is to be wary of. He is playing his cards very close.'

Mitch dismisses what Katrin has said. 'I'll see what happens to you before I make a move.'

The JESTER speaks.

Hmm, the businessman chooses caution. I wonder how the Queen will react? The Knave is manipulating the model well. See how he plays them, as he would pawns. But this move may be to the Queen's advantage. Not exactly Chess, but keep the idea in your head.

Phil picks up on the conversation. 'I wonder where Pablo got to? I have a feeling him walking off was a bad move.'

Alain cannot resist himself 'I think he went down there. I'm sure he took my food stash.'
Phil announces another voicemail coming in...... 'do you only consider your own belly? Have you ever stopped to think of those who may not even get a single meal a day? Perhaps you should experience life in another place, the Yemen perhaps.' Alain throws up his hands and blows out a loud breath. 'What, who is doing this?'

Katrin is puzzled by the geometry of the void. It takes no obvious form and apart from what appears to be an exit either side (judging by the movements of Gabriella and Pablo) the existence of the sun moving from west to east is challenging Katrin's instinct and intellect. 'He went down there. I'll go take a look. Give me a few minutes.' Katrin walks away. She walks only a few metres before the way in front of her is completely transformed. 'Whoa, what is this?'

Padre Alfonso has been standing and observing events within the void and that voice inside his head plagues him again. This time he cannot contain it and shouts angrily. 'Why are we being tormented with the voices? What trick is God playing on us?' He clenches his fist and continues. 'I have lived a simple life, observing the scriptures, making no demands. Life taken from my sister because of some human virus, my calling brought into question by zealots and sinners. And now we are in the desert seeing the sands shifting. 40 days and 40 nights? Is this our time of preparation as our good lord did? In what more ways shall we be tested or tempted? Sirens, the fates, what type of hell is this? Is there no restitution?'

Phil tries to confide in him. 'Be careful padre, the temptation is already with us. We are in the midst of a battle in time and forces are playing us.'

But Padre Alfonso has lost any sense of consideration or acknowledgement for what has been said. In his fury he erupts. 'Since when did you have power of insight? No mortal can see into the future. You are a heretic, you are the anti-christ. You, along with those who lust, who lie with their own kind, along with those who kill the unborn. You shall be judged!'

And with that he storms off, pushing Phil aside and heads away from the group. The low light of the void grows darker until no-one can see one another.

Pablo Mendes didn't have to walk for long before he found himself out of the void and in a space occupied by a white statue. He didn't think to question it because, there, the most beautiful woman he ever saw was mounted on a pedestal. Her eyes gazed on him and they seemed to be following him as he walked around lusting at her and being consumed by her beauty. He couldn't help giving out a wolf whistle and, breathing heavily he mutters, 'look at you, we could make good times together.' He leans closer to her face, and hears a voice say 'I am Atropos', when a tear of blood runs down the cheek of the statue. 'Que? How …?' In disbelief he touches her face, smearing blood over it and his hands. He jumps as Padre Alfonso comes up behind him.

'You! You dare to approach her? Her beauty, her presence? It is our blessed lady. Blessed be her name. The Lord is with thee.'   'What are you talking about, old man. You are nuts. Have you not seen this? That statue is crying bloody tears!' He holds his stained hands up as proof. Padre Alfonso yells in a rage 'You show your act? How corrupted has one to be, that the devil himself dares to show himself through him? You wretched foul!'

'Woah, steady, I didn't do anything? It's a statue!' Padre hears none of this.'It is the miracle of her! And you defiled it!' And in that anger and rage he tackles the shocked Mendes and with his rosary throws his hands around his neck. 'You will pay for what you have done! You filth! Evil I see in your eyes! The devil! DIE!'   Alfonso tightens the rosary around his neck and breathing wildly twists the rosary tight. A moment later Mendes rolls his eyes back. He is dead. The Padre steps off his victim, realizing what he has done. He looks at his hands, that now are bruised and scratched and then to the statue's face – which has no more blood at all. 'My GOD, my GOD. What have I done?' He runs off thrusting his rosary in his deep pocket.

The Knave speaks out to the Queen << You've taken one of mine, I knew he was struggling, but in so doing you have guaranteed the end of the cleric, a piece for a piece madam>>

The Queen retorts   'That wasn't my move. If I remember rightly, your gripe is with the King.'

Katrin enters the grey space that is the crime scene. There is no statue. There is no blood. Just the body of Pablo Mendes, with a thread of finest silk wrapped around his neck. 'What in the …? Help! HELP!'

The void starts to light up again to its former situation and a low mist settles. Within seconds she returns to the group…clearly distressed. 'I've just found Pablo Mendes. He's dead. Garotted. White as a sheet.'

The JESTER speaks

Another move. Methinks someone is getting angry and impatient.

Alain speaks first. 'So who's the culprit? Let's show our hand eh? Who spins the wheel?'

The JESTER speaks

Talk about mixed metaphors? I wonder what kind of game he thinks we are playing? I don't think the chef is up to this. Way beyond his pay grade. Not a good choice for the King.

'He was holding this.' Katrin holds up a collection of papers.

'It says…..US businesses start to panic as African states measure up in the supply of silicon to the hi-tech giants of Seattle.

North African countries, led by Morocco are dictating terms to US giants Cyclops and Synergen Inc. As they become aware of their bargaining position in a time of dwindling supply of rare material to feed the incessant IT belly, these countries are increasingly raising issues of ecology and sustainability as bargaining chips. Amidst this new game changer, ecologists and environmentalists are observing unusual weather patterns in the Sahara region and note the recent massive dust storm which sent orange clouds over parts of southern Europe, followed by heavy rains, the first recorded rains in the area for over a thousand years.'

Mitch shouts out. 'Utter baloney. Fake news. From China. Cyclops is not in difficulty. Headline profits will be announced soon. And, hey, heavy rains, when did we experiece heavy rains?'

Phil speaks. 'We have a murderer among us and all you can be bothered to do is read a business paper and talk of profit?'

Katrin picks up on an earlier conversation. 'There's something in what Phil is saying. Something big, almost metaphysical is happening and we seem to have been drawn into it. Why would someone want to kill off Mendes? Why are we getting voicemail messages about some aspect of our past? And don't be pointing the finger at me. I found him, I had no grudge against the man.'

Alain. 'Me neither. He spoke to me before we got into this hole, told me that there were people in his country prepared to go to extreme lengths to obtain silicon in order to do deals with the IT giants…..God I'm hungry.'

The Knave speaks. <<I have as much time as eternity but I grow impatient, and, if I'm honest a trifle bored. Let's step up the play. Knight, make a move>>

The knight reacts surprisingly. Oh, am I on? Right. Let's see. Ummm, Rook 7 to Cleric 5 . There, that takes the POLITICIAN out.

<<Not a wise move foolish knight. He was already lost>>

The Queen responds to the Knave's comment 'We play at my speed, in my time. But, so be it. The King can afford to lose a few more if they are not to change heart. And the POLITICIAN was rotten to the core, not much hope of redemption there. But I tried, a long time ago. Here's one for the ARCHITECT.'

Phil checks his mobile phone. Another voicemail..... 'You maintain your manifest certainty in the design of your building, ARCHITECT. In your pride you failed to see that your design could not and would not withstand the extremes of weather being witnessed in the Sahara. Neither did you properly investigate concerns from the landowners and construction company about water flows and underground streams, dismissing them as mere peasants. There were design flaws. A pinch of humility would not go amiss.'

The JESTER speaks

A good move by the the Queen. Let's see if she takes the bite.

Katrin bows her head and quietly trembles. 'Something tells me we have to work at something, and work together to get over this.'

Phil. 'Seems to me we are in the middle of a time warp. No, seriously, and no sarcastic comments about a 1970's dance move either. We are in some weird metaphysical time storm or battle. A battle between the past, present and future. I didn't want to say anything, but last night I had a nightmare…'

The JESTER speaks

This looks promising.

'Maybe I had a vision. It flashed in front of me. An hourglass type object with sand running down. Only the hourglass was on its side.The sand depicting time, and time was running out. We were stuck in the middle of the hourglass, unsure of which way to go. Do we follow the sand or do we try to resist it? And something was pushing us to go in different directions. And outside the hourglass was an eye, a huge eye watching everything, everywhere. And the eye was laughing!'

Alain howls 'You've completely lost it pal. I had a vision too… me eating something other than a bloody meat tagine…haahaha
And the murder? What's that about O man of vision?'

Phil. 'Well it wasn't me. I don't know, maybe it's part of a test?'

Alfonso keeps his bruised hands inside his deep pockets and struggles to gesticulate without them. Nevertheless he still manages to shout 'You are all crazy. Visions, tests, time…if anyone should have a vision it ought to be me.'

Phil 'Oh bleeding hell, another voicemail.... thou shalt not kill. Well, whatever it is I fear it is getting stronger. The voices are becoming more intense.' His voice speaks to him: *'Yes they are.'*

Katrin plucks up some semblance of courage to speak. 'You know I like music, right? Well.....no, please just hear me out. I had a dream a few days before we set out on the trek. And the dream featured the song Woodstock in which Joni Mitchell sings 'and we've got to get ourselves back to the garden.' It's a metaphor. It's about how the world has got screwed up and we have a duty to restore the balance. It's about us.'

Mitch shakes his head and jeers angrily 'So? What, so now you're uttering some 1970's hippie mantra. Get a life woman. You'll be advocating we sit in the lotus position next.'

Phil reacts excitedly.'She's right. At last someone is on my wavelength.'

Katrin gives Mitch two fingers and continues. 'That nightmare, these happenings. All linked. We are all being tested to face our demons and only by doing this will we ever get out of here, and restore balance. These cellphone messages are pointers.'

The Knave murmurs to himself <<Oh, she is good, very good. I'm not sure if I can maintain control over her. The King picked a smart one there. Maybe the best piece on the board. Let me play the BUSINESSMAN again>>

Mitch. 'You are nuts. Complete rubbish, woman. And as for him, 'THE BLOGGER', well he's too lazy to even change his clothes and have a wash. And you call him a visionary. Give me a break.'

The Queen takes a deep breath and speaks to the group.

'You fell asleep in one world, and woke up in another. I gave you heaven, you bathed in my waters. But I'll give you hell...... out there... in the world......your world, this time:

Paris is no longer romantic,

New York, the city that never sleeps, now sleeps

No one walks the Great Wall

Sydney plays no opera and Mecca is silent of prayer.

Hugs & kisses have become weapons, and keeping your distance has become an act of love.

Suddenly you humans are realising that power, beauty & money are worthless, and can't get you the oxygen you're fighting for.

I say ....you are not necessary. The air, earth, water and sky without you are fine. When you come back if you ever do, remember that you are my guests. Not my masters. I will save myself, with or without your assistance.'

The Knave shouts. <<Right. You want to play dirty, I'll show you dirty>>

The Queen responds 'You haven't heard the half of it.' The group look up and at each other, completely dumbfounded by what they hear.

CHAPTER 13

THE LABYRINTH GARDEN

The Queen runs through a corridor of thin veils. 'Cursed! Virtue this and virtue that. What virtue is worth the salt against the sin of man? Tears upon tears!' She stops in front of a fractured mirror-mosaic and looks upon herself.

'What hath beauty ever brought but withering? Mortals. Sent by the the King, to help me or ruin me? They're getting closer by sheer will, not by what is right. Soon they must find my inner sanctum in this dead kingdom. My garden, my secret. But make no mistake, if they dare to act vile within my sanctuary, in this prison, I will let them have wrath even unknown to hell and hellfire! My children! Let virtue be virtue and sin be sin, this is where I draw the line!' She takes a shard of the mirror and cuts her hand. Blood is dripping into the sand, where saplings grow into green meadows.

'My blood be spilled in thine name! The King, you could have sent more virtuous mortals. More blood to spill on top of this.' And she walks away.

....

Alain shakes his head, scratches it and wonders how he has now found himself barging down an alameda of palm trees, picking up a fermented date - getting drunk and three sheets to the wind. His walk is unsteady and he laughs inanely.
'Ma chere! Ma chere! Sweet are the fruits! Not sour and spoiled. Clean and ripe just to pick up. What is this paradise in the middle of the desert? If I could import those ingredients, they would run in the doors of my restaurant. The critics would have to bite their tongue! I could show them all. Again! *(hicks)* Marcel Alain! Finest THE CHEF! Three stars – every year!'

He stops and throws one of the dates into a fountain. The surface ruffling his reflection. He looks into the liquid which is still and shining. 'What have you done with your life? With your genius, batton Alain! I have lost the feel for good food. So many dishes wasted upon wealthy pigs, pearls thrown in front of them. My cuisine lost heart. Ma couer! I'm nothing but in denial and depraved of passion. But this .. THIS is a new beginning! More, more, more!'

He stands up confident to speak his will to the heavens and seal it, but being drunk instead he stumbles over a balustrade, falling over the side. He lands with a thud. 'Ouch, oh shit where now.'
It smells damp, moist, earthly. Light is absent. Big roots ranking from above into the ground give off a vague glow. Shadows rule here and silence. The world rests in peace. He gets himself up, dusting off. 'Merde. I must've tripped. Ough, my head. Where am I?'
Two eyes in the dark come forward. 'You're at the end, compadre.'   'The end?'

'Si, the place, where no moves are left. Where all your options are played. This is the realm of the dead and just to be born. Underneath the garden of the world. She – las muerres - buries the dead – la muerrto. I can vouch for it.'

The two eyes step out of the dark and it is the dead POLITICIAN.

Alain recoils in surprise. 'Mon dieu, we thought you were dead! Killed! What are you doing here?'
'You're not listening Amigo - I am dead. I was killed – by her wrath … The question is what are you doing here? You smell of booze – and the dead don't drink. Believe me I've tried.'

Alain tries to take in what has been said, hicks and slurs 'The dead? Oh no no no no – I ain't dead, my head is hurting. I'm in pain. I have ambitions, again – will. Life in me. How can I be dead? A second ago I was in this beautiful garden, closer to life than ever and now? The underworld? Merde! Zut alors!'

'We both have been tricked. Well, I guess we were warned but shit, who's listening? Could have been better. But not for us, it wasn't. We were invited to the party, but never welcome. That is the way with her. Unless you work on her terms. That is where I failed up there, in life. If the fruits are hanging too high, you're supposed to grow – not to bring the fruits down. I always forced my way onto beauty and took it – that was my demise. I missed the consent and now she rejected me forever. I can never return.'

Alain snorts loudly and a piece of snot and spit shoots out from his face. 'Pah, weirdo. I know your kind – with your pathos and big speeches. You're still just a horny dog. But me? I was honest. Humble. Celebrated beauty in devotion, in taste. I served her, her garden. I cooked with my heart – and always hated men like you, that never listened. Never said thank you – only demanding. Power and riches, for doing nothing. No sacrifice. For you it is fair – for me not! I will find a way back! I deserve it! I still have a kitchen to run! Look at me Ma, top of the world! Adieu!'   He walks away only to turn back and walk in the opposite direction.

'Good luck, compadre. Not many Langoustines where you're going.' And the two eyes turn back into the shadows.

....

Gabriella walks under the blossoming jasmin, feeling young and fresh. With a light step she inhales the fresh air. 'Ahhhh. This place is so beautiful! Super cool. I'm glad I went upside. Better take a picture of me!' She takes a selfie. 'If only I could live here forever. Maybe they have panini and a chai latte? Service is really frustrating.'

A wind gushes through the jasmin, leaves falling all around. They turn into a beautiful woman: the Queen. 'Are you not satisfied with what I have to offer?'

Gabriella looks on in awe 'Woah, sry I didn't mean to … actually I was talking about somebody else. I mean look at you 'hello'? How awesome is that dress. You got it for a promo? Nice catch there, Ma'am!'

'Ma'am?' The sky darkens for a split second, as her voice echoes like thunder. 'How old do I look for you?'
'Oops, I'm sry – I'm such a clutz …'

'Please … do us both a favour and stop it with the big eyes! I'm not one of your tools from you haute coutur handbag. And I'm certainly not your camera.'

Gabriella faces the Queen and gesticulates with her hands and neck. 'Uh, here come the claws. Like, how do you know about me?'

'Shut your jaw. I'm here to do you a big favour.'

'Oh, and what could that be?'

'Showing you your true self for once. No filters, no bubble – just you.'

Gabriella is non plussed 'Okay, I get it. You're like one of those spiritual media influencers, wanna sell me your self-help book now? All this new age crap is so '90s. Doesn't get followers nowadays. You should like consider switching to fitness and cleansing.'

The Queen steps back and spends a second in thought. She speaks again. 'You're quite a piece of work. But see for yourself ...' The Queen picks a jasmin blossom and hands it to Gabriella. As the blossom opens it reveals a mirror. She is shocked to see an old woman as her reflection. Hair grey, wrinkles – but clearly it is her.

Gabriella winces back. 'Ewww! I'm old, I look like a dried grape. I know those apps, it's a cool effect, but I don't want to see that.'

'But you have to - beauty is a curse and your true ……'

Gabriella cuts her off   'Yo, for F's sake - are you stuck in the 1950s? Enough with the body shaming - I don't have to do ... anything. This is like my body and it is awesome no matter what. I don't have to be afraid of that. Take the high road, Bettsy. You make the same mistake as all the other first generation emancipators. You trade one burden with another. First we women should be devoted to our husbands, JUSTA LIKEA MY MAMMA.
And now we should be devoted to ourselves and virtue.
What if I don't want to be devoted to anyone. Not to you, not the men and not to myself. Maybe I want to be in tune with what I am once. Not being ashamed for my looks, my privilege or my place in this world. How about that!

And this isn't about me, right? This is about you. You wanna be free and you wanna be emancipated, getting away from your husband and boring homelife. Well let me tell you break free of that cage all you want, if you're not free from yourself - you'll never be. Eat, pray, love is just another golden cage. You can be a prisoner of ourself, just as you can be of another. If you wanna break free you have to realize: You are already free, you're just not living it.'

The Queen looks at the MODEL open-mouthed.

'Yeah! Unclench that ...!'

Now the Queen cuts in 'My, firm and resolute, you've come on well on your journey. I'm almost impressed. But that is still not a way to talk to a Queen.'

'Yay, sorry. So who's you?'

The Queen passes a comment to herself 'Hmmm, maybe that young, naive damsel is right.'

Gabriella struts, bag on her shoulder 'Hello, Hey, I'm standing right here!'

'Yes, you are. So ... why? You seem to have figured it all out. And as you said, a modern woman doesn't need a King or a Queen. So, why are you here? Perhaps we will find out later.' And with that the Queen disappears as quickly as she emerged.

Gabriella. 'Hey, whoah, come back you still haven't told me who you are.'

....

Padre Alfonso hears loud thumping in his head. He sees colours and mist. Rooks and crows sqwak as if some bird of prey is trying to steal the baby chicks. He flees into the sunken temple of the kingdom. Flees from what he has done. From his murder, from his sin. He kneels down, sobbing. 'What have I done? I killed a man. Killed! But how, I didn't plan for it. I had no grudge against this man. I didn't even know him, some hours ago. How long?'

In front of him is a withered statue of the former idol of the temple. It is Atropos. Barely distinguishable from a pillar. Suddenly Cassim emerges out of the silhouette. 'Oh suck it up.' The skeleton slaps the padre hard on the face. 'Get up.' Padre Alfonso lets out a gargled scream 'The devil, death! Hell hath come!'

'That's what I hated most about the priestly role - you cannot help it, can you? Accepting, that you are in charge - you and nobody else.'

Alfonso rests on one knee, his hands clenched and he beats his head. 'How can I be responsible if I was possessed by some form of demon? By hate, burning in my heart - nothing could contain it.'

Cassim eyes him dismissively. 'Life and suffering always riddled you, which made you uncertain, which built fear, which made you devoted, which made you small-hearted. All the million, million times you found solace in god - were a million, million small steps in the wrong direction. Away from fear, away from truth. And now you have paid the price. For being a coward in front of your own heart. You called it belief - but it was just a napkin for the little boy that kept running back from cruel life.'

Alfonso composes himself, stands up and confronts the skeleton frame. 'You call me a coward for that? To struggle with this fallen world? To not understand it? To search for a way that would explain the cruelty of the world with a higher framing, where there is no cruelty. A hope, that there is a plain of existence without suffering, that supersedes what we mortals experience here? You call me a coward for that?'

'Believe me, I've been around a while and have the stretch marks to prove it… well, maybe not any more. I know what life, and death is. Because, there is only one life that matters. And that is now. Here. With all the suffering, with all the fight, with all the doubt. With all the sins we've committed. Own up to it. Learn from it. What is done, is done. You're still a padre. A man of guidance - now guide them. Otherwise all is lost.'

'How can I guide them, if I was the one who failed in the first place? And who are you to lecture me on what I should or should not do….are you the voice I heard those weeks ago that left me in so much pain? Who tells me you're not one of those playing their games with us. Another idol - another false prophet? Why should I trust you, if you tell me to trust none?'

'Perhaps you are right. I was the master of lies a long time ago. Maybe I was the one furthest away from the truth. Maybe I came back.
But as for you, well, yes, you failed - congratulations - now you're one step less further away from the truth. For you, I'm afraid there is no way out.' With that he vanishes into the stone again.

…………………..

The Knave rides through the labyrinth. Not looking left or right, when suddenly someone stands in his way, leaning on a pillar. It is Mitch. 'Hello, hello, hello. So you're the bad guy?'

The Knave looks, squinting his eyes. <<You insect! Fear my blade, to conquest!>>

Mitch waves a hand, checks his watch and sits on a rock. 'Come on, who're ya kiddin'? There is no army here. You're not fighting a fight - you're looting a corpse. I get it: hostile take-over. But from one professional to another: Boy, your performance lacks ambition.'

<<Who are you to dare speak to me in this manner - I'll have your tongue cut out!>>

'No, I don't think you will - because I'm the only who can help you.'

<<You?! Ahahahahahahah! Jocosely! I'm the Knave - the only one who conquered the realm of the dead - entered it's gate by trial. I've wandered for years, fought armies and laid bare the treasures of many powerful men to gain entrance. It's been a long journey. You're just ... a fluke of destiny. One of his lackies. A spectator, not a contender. So get out off my way!>>

Mitch feels he is just getting into his stride. Brimming with self confidence, he lets loose. 'I would get out of your way ... If you'd have any. But you're lost. No fire, just hot air. Perhaps you truly did all those things - as you said you're a contender. But you're no mortal. Whatever your agenda is. That is the difference between me and the rest - I'm a winner. I don't play the freaking games. I see something I want - I'll go straight for the price. And that is something you can't do. Can ya?'

<<No mortal can cheat death. Now ... move on and let me pass. I have bigger fish to fry, to use your mortal terms>>   The Knave trots on, with his horse.
Mitch gathers the harness and halts the beast. 'Have you seen him?' The Knave halts, looks down and rolls his eyes << Have I seen who?>>

'The King, of course. Your opponent - the former champion. I bet you haven't, have ya! Do you know why?'

<<Enlighten me. What King?>> The Knave moves his eyes as if to puzzle over the businessman's knowledge.

'Because the King is long as dead as this whole sand worn kingdom. Stuck in the castle, hardly made a move. Expecting us to do his work for him. And even he doesn't know what I know. There is only the one jumping around, alive and well - doing all his business. The one, who has all of us fooled. Or so he thinks.'

There is a moment of silence as the Knave tries to comprehend how the businessman knows so much. He doesn't recall any mention of a king at any previous time. He wonders whether he knows more. <<Make your point. I concede nothing>>

'Every power has a source. And we know who can hop in and out of this place. Who is having us jump through the hoops. If you really wanna win the game - corrupt the referee …'

....

Katrin and Phil have found themselves in a huge walled garden. There are trees and knarled roots everywhere wrapped around. Relics of ancient statues are distorted and the roots entwine them. It would suggest of something religious possibly, but most certainly something revered… once.
Phil. 'Hey look, we can see the night sky from here …' Katrin replies, looking at the architecture.
'Yeah, I don't think I'm up for poetic nonsense, right now.'
'No, - that's not … It proves a point. Think of this place as a simulation - a black box - right …'
'Okay, so….'

'We have been disconnected from the outside world - no call, no visuals, no reference of time. Everything was blocked, like the law of physics tight. But, if we can see starlight - that means, there is information leaking into the simulation. That means there is a way back. There is hope!'

Katrin considers his observation. 'Hmmm, sounds reasonable. However, if we're stranded in a side pocket of reality - somebody has to run the simulation - and has to run it on something. A dream needs a dreamer and memory it can build on.' They walk to the centre of the square, where an old weaving loom lies, the threads cast around randomly.

'Katrin, you build things, right? Where are the most important places in any building?'

'Well, pivotal points - structural nodes. Focal vectors …'

'Yeah ...OK. I meant the middle. The centre.'

'Oh, sure.'

Phil continues. 'Where we came from, whatever place that was, there were only two entrances or exits. But here, there is a north, south, west and east entrance. It's the middle of the labyrinth. We're at the centre of whatever is going on. And this ... loom or whatever is pivotal to the solution. Jeez, Crap, No. *Yes you've found it*. Go away. Not now I'm talking with the architect. *Keep it to yourself.'* Phil paces around shaking his head and flicking his fingers.

Katrin. 'Hey are you OK?'

Phil tries to compose himself… 'Uhhhh, yeah. Somewhere in here….. I saw a vision, maybe even a nightmare….. a huge crucifix standing, being held in place by the finest of thread, but the thread is choking it. And on the top of the cross a huge all seeing eye. God it was like like seeing the new testament, Homer and Tolkien all rolled up……

It's a loom, but it ran out of thread. That's why we're stuck here. The machine is broke.'

Katrin looks on, confused. 'So, what do you suggest? You suggest we untangle it, but how? There is no way through this mess! If we cut the wrong root, everything could wither. All that is left. I mean, look what happened to that Colombian guy.'

Phil. 'You remember that message the Spanish model got…. check your personality, and then you said something, I dunno, about a band, and then you mentioned three fates…. well didn't they weave from a loom? Wasn't it something from Greek mythology?'

Katrin. 'It's like all the different belief systems rallying together. Well perhaps not all of them… a mix of the religious and the other worldly. But what does it all mean?'

Phil. 'We have to look beyond - it's a dream. The loom is that which runs the place - the fates. It is the thoughts that run the loom and the feelings that run the heart. Wake up, we're in the realm of the spirits, logic is only half true here. You have to imagine as well as measure. You have to believe your heart and follow it.'

Katrin. 'I wish I could. But what about you, you seem to have the knowledge. Must say it's come as a surprise. I thought all that earlier stuff was just mumbo jumbo. I'm sorry.'

Phil. 'No worries. Well there is only one way to find out. But I don't think I'm quite ready yet…'

CHAPTER 14

ALL RISE - DISORDER IN COURT

The Jester calls the Queen and Knave to order. 'Excuse me, hello. One moment please. If I may be of help. Perhaps we should just review where things are at this moment in time. It seems to me that certain points of order need to be resolved before matters get out of hand.'

The JESTER speaks

They couldn't hear me before but they certainly can now.

The Queen speaks. ' Goodness, why, it's you. Long time no see. You haven't changed in several million years. All right. I'm comfortable with that. Though I've made my points abundantly clear to everyone in one way or another.'

The Knave speaks to the Jester.... <<Do I know you? Are you able to do this? I wasn't aware you had authority to intercede. And, by the way, how does the businessman know about you?>>

'Oh, I'm merely a facilitator, but I think it might be an idea to consider your battle lines and future strategy. Anything requiring a decision will have to go to a higher authority.'

The Knave and Queen both cut in. 'So be it.'

'I will have to speak through the remains of the old crony Cassim.' He speaks up to the roof of the void... 'Sire, I seek a favour.'
The King awakes from a slumber and is clearly annoyed that his peace has been disturbed. '.... What now, Cassim?'

'Sire, I am speaking through your wizened old skeleton, Cassim. 'Tis the JESTER Arcadeus. Remember me? You are no doubt aware that ummm…events……ummm in the Sahara are rather turbulent right now and I am requesting you to temporarily freeze time as far as these humans are concerned, so our protagonists can re-assess their strategies. Without too much audacity on my part Sire, it shouldn't be tricky: the sand clock is already on it's side. No doubt you want it righted?'

'Freeze time? And you, the court fool. Who are you to demand I freeze time?'

'Sire, I am a mere facilitator and I demand nothing, 'cept to intercede for the world and the metaphysical world. It would seem to be a move that would be to your advantage and potentially bring the drama to a solution suitable to all concerned.'

Cassim tries to over-ride the voice of the jester. 'Tis I sire, Cassim. I think it would be a good strategy, not a specific move on your part, but a good strategy. You would be giving nothing away.'

'This is all very confusing. And still no final push to my throne. Are you tired Knave, searching for a route in or just given up? And you are a couple of knights down.'

The Knave. <<One must make sacrifices to reach a preferred solution>>

'Indeed. Time is frozen. Temporarily. I'm going to resume my nap. Wake me up if anything significant occurs.'

The Queen taps her heels, impatiently. 'So, JESTER. What is your agenda?'

'I have <u>no</u> agenda. I was of the view that the game might be about to get dirty. I'm bound to make sure you BOTH respect the rules. And the King is two pieces down. Not that it is my concern.'

The JESTER speaks

I think I've got my work cut out. I may be some time.

The Knave speaks. <<So, Queen of the desert, where do you want this to go and how much do you desire the flag of conquest? Remember, my war is with the King, not you. The King sleeps in his ruined castle and we make the sacrifices. Why not let it all go? Do you think he has a care for you? After all it is he who is primus inter pares; you can only be second best. Let me take him>>

She replies. 'It was he who summoned the humans against you and your knights. Your desire was and still is, is to interfere with the sands of time. My motives are pure. To allow the earth to breathe, to allow the passage of time to pass freely. You have manipulated the mortals to behave with free will and abandon the universal truths, thus I will fulfil my pledge with or without their help. After all, I have the Moires to call upon and they have executed their duties most adequately.'

The Jester intercedes. 'Getting anywhere?'

'I think not. The Knave wishes me to lay aside my sirens and step down. I'll have none of it. In fact I'm tempted to whip up a mother of all storms.'

'Belay there, oh Queen. Sire, If I may offer an idea?'
The Queen and the Knave face each other.'Yes, proceed.'

The Jester again. 'Why not test the mortals as to their inner desires and motives and make yourselves known to them, such that the outcome determines the way ahead.'

The Queen sniffs dismissively. 'Hmm, I thought I had done that already.'

And the Knave concurs 'Me too and I'm curious about that businessman…where on earth did that old King find him?'

The Jester pauses, sighs quietly to himself and continues …. 'Yes, OK, look. Neither of you have made yourselves known to them, personally so to speak. You have spoken to them only through the medium of the voicemail and then in the labyrinth. A most confusing attempt might I say?'

The Knave <<Pah, the cheek of it. And from a court jester too. So, and how would we do this?>>

'By the machinery of the court. Stretch their intelligence. But I think you may have to concede some of your raison d'etre. It will be, in human words, a mindshift of epic proportion.'

Now the Queen has her say. 'And if we choose the court, who will judge. Who will be the jury? Tried by one's peers?'

<<Perhaps the jury is the world in all its glory. Perhaps the outcome itself will determine the guilty or not guilty verdict. We may be at odds but we must agree on one thing. If we reveal the plot too early they'll surely not play the game. Some know more than others already>>

The Queen responds. 'Yes, I see your point. Let's play the mortals some more. But, Knave do not try to bend the rules.'

<<So be it>>

The Jester speaks again, via Cassim. 'Sire, 'tis Arcadeus. We appear to have made an arrangement. You can unfreeze time.'

'Done, but watch that Knave, he plays by his own rules. And his moves are crafty. By the way, I haven't been asleep the whole time. I watched your driving back there. Not bad for a court fool.'

Gabriella returns to the group, well what is left of them. She speaks. 'I travelled upside, and I don't know where it took me but I'm like back here with you lot. And I've completely lost my sense of time. Where are we now? It looked like some weird garden or park, with lots of wall and flowers and stuff. Posh ladee too.'

The voice of Alain speaks out. 'Seemed to resemble a maze. I suppose it's something like a maze garden? I dunno. Great plonk.'   Nobody can hear him apart from the Queen.

The Queen. 'You are in Sahara Time mortals. You are here not by chance or physical choice. You are here to fulfil a task.'

Gabriella 'Ah, here she is...'

Phil. 'It's her......I knew it, *You knew it all along*. They wouldn't believe me would they?
No they wouldn't. You were always right.'
Mitch. 'And who are you, Madam?'

'If you can comprehend the idea, mortal, I am the Queen, I am Earth. I am in balance. That is, I <u>was</u> in balance until he, the Knave thought to despoil me and the the King. But I am also the prosecution.'

Katrin. 'So, was it <u>you</u> who made all this world chaos happen...floods, virus pandemics, earthquakes and ice caps melting?'

'I had a bit of a hand in it. Well, yes it was my handiwork. But do not call it chaos.'

Alain's voice again 'And the murder of the POLITICIAN? Excuse me, the murder, duuhhh?'

The Queen speaks aside to the chef. 'Let's just say that was a bad move. On his part.'

The Knave can't resist <<Didn't help the King, did it!>>   And then he turns his attention to the group. <<Now you 5 must walk the road as horizons change and let the tournament continue. By the way I'm your best defence>>

Mitch. 'What sort of perverted tournament are you referring to? Hey c'mon people, why aren't you saying something?'

The Queen casts a gaze on the businessman and ponders. 'You have left the physical world and entered the world of the metaphysical.'

Gabriella chips in for good measure. 'Is this like us being in Game of Thrones? Joking.... but listen. Where I was. Oh it was beautiful. Like I imagine the hanging gardens of Babylon. Wish I had a garden like that. Such beautiful flowers. Oh hey, where's that POLITICIAN guy, and the CHEF?

Didn't like either of them, that Colombian like he was coming on to me big style. Did someone say murder?'

Padre. 'He's dead. Someone garrotted him''. 'Someone grotted him? Wassatt?'

'He was strangled, young lady. As for the chef, nobody knows. Perhaps he was the culprit.'

Katrin. 'Mebbee. I guess we are all suspect. I don't know how to explain all this but I found myself with Phil here in some strange walled garden with statues and twisted roots. Something similar to Angkor Wat, in Cambodia. You know? But nothing like as big. And there in the very centre... a loom. An interesting design.
But I could not and still cannot see its inherent purpose, it's logic. Is it to puzzle us or to lead us?' She thinks to herself. I think I could have done better. Then she thinks again.
Wait, no. This is not the way to go. Am I being played here? Am I supposed to bathe is some sort of professional pride, and in so doing rubbish all before me? And then she resumes, pleading to the group. 'Listen, we are being played on our vices. Do not fall into the trap.'

'Give me a sign, oh Lord. Show me which way to go. Alone in this desert with the devils, heretics and fornicators around me.' Alfonso looks up and holds his hands in the air.... 'Da sihi mignum' *(give me the sign)*.

Now Phil. 'A virus has already struck. Our phones are dead. Nothing going out. Voices coming in.'
The Queen focuses her energies on Phil. 'So when are you going to get out of your dump and do something about this? All very well having insight but you need to use it be able to deal with it. Face it, you saw the future, you didn't like it but you're too lazy to do anything about it. And as for

saving your fellow travellers, well forget that one. That would require an element of community spirit on your part.'

Phil turns away from the group, looking up to try and catch a sight of the Queen. He is shaking his head, his fingers are twiddling and he cannot keep still. He starts to talk to himself and his alter ego talks back to him with a menacing sneer.

'Look, I kept you quiet to protect you. I thought you and I were friends.

No we were never friends. I just led you along.

But you helped me confirm all that is happening.

No, I led you here.

But what about all the stuff to do with the Moires and so on?

If you want to know everything you must go back and find the centre of the maze. And don't bother with Online maps either. Face it, the power of IT is useless in here. Knowledge is power, and in the physical world where you belong, Online has usurped knowledge and devalued it. Use your brain, you idiot.'

Alain is slurring badly and his vision is blurred. 'Man. That fruit wash strong. I can't get enough of it. Hey, can anyone hear me?'

Gabriella turns to face the Queen. 'So if you're prosecuting, what's the crime? What have we done. A murder? All this way to be tried for murder? What else could happen in the desert?'

She changes the emphasis. 'Maybe a magic carpet ride? A whole new world, haha. A modelling contract. Pah, but I don't have the looks of Princess Jasmine. Maybe the secret of the maze will give me eternal good looks. Whadya say Jose?' She looks around pathetically. No one returns the look.

The Queen changes her tone to try and get inside Gabriella. 'It's what's on the inside that counts.'

It didn't work. The Knave hears everything. He shouts loudly, shaking the area. <<Don't believe that. If looks could kill they probably will>>

Katrin. 'Hey that's a line from Peter Gabriel's 'Games without Frontiers.' Using non military people to fight a non military war. A war of ideologies, of 'isms.' Is that us? Is that why we're here?'

The Queen smiles and nods appreciatively. 'It is, intelligent mortal. And so is this.....

Downside up

Upside down

Take my weight off the ground

Falling deep in the sky

Slipping into the unknown....'

Katrin. 'So you sent that text message?'   Queen. 'Yes. It was me actually.'

The Knave. <<You know it's meaning, don't you?>>

'Well I can't say for sure, but my interpretation is it is about a life in the non physical world. Looking up to the Earth from the sky below.'

<<You are the most intelligent of the 7. It was a warning to you of the consequences>>
Mitch didn't like the manner of that last remark. He gazes at his watch. He notices that throughout the time they have been in this void his watch has continued to work as normal. He's intrigued. He

looks at the Knave. 'Umm, hey, sorry about all that rage earlier. I wonder if I could have a private word with one of you?'

The Knave. <<Shoot>>

'I was hoping to get the Queen's attention. Look, who is in control here? I see complete chaos.'

The Knave, offended by such a dismissal replies. <<You see what you want to see. It could be your greatest desire or your worst nightmare>>

Mitch again. 'Look, we're decent people, you and me, is there some way you and I could, maybe, like strike a deal to get me outa here?'

The Knave. <<That would be against the rules. Which I am prepared to bend, but not on this occasion friend>>

'But I know that the BLOGGER possesses knowledge. He could be of harm to you. I can help you in his downfall. And I know what is going on behind the scenes. Time is being played. I warned you earlier. You should not cross me.'

The Knave cocks his head, checks his sword and scoffs loudly. 'His downfall is already written. Knight 2, make a move. Challenge the BLOGGER but do not take him out yet.'

In the background Alfonso has started to tremble. 'I was at the centre. I found a tomb but the stone had moved. The tomb- empty. And the statue of our lady. What sign is this? Insanus sum ego vado' *(I am going crazy).*

He rips off his rosary and screws it around his fist, then starts to beat his chest. The others look on wide eyed and speechless but are reluctant to intervene. Except Gabriella. She goes up to him and gives him a comforting stroke to his back. 'We'll find a way out, Padre, have faith.'
He breaks down in tears.

The JESTER speaks

Oops, looks like the cleric is about to go off the board if I'm not mistaken. We've already said 'Adieu' to the chef and the politician. The theatre of the absurd appears to be turning into a theatre of war.

Phil…speaks to himself. 'So there's a Queen, a Knave, a Jester. Where is the King in this bizarre game we play?'

Cassim replies, but only Phil can hear. "I am Cassim. I speak for the King."

Phil. 'Can you tell me what are the King's intentions?' Cassim. 'If I tell you, you will surely go mad.' Phil. 'I'm already there. Tell me.'

'He has created a virus of illusion. He means to take back his Queen by any means. It is he who controls the passage of time and the Knave seeks to change the very essence of time itself. He has brought you all here to strengthen his campaign. You could change everything……and stop the virus spreading. Now tell the others.'
Phil runs to the centre of the group, eyes wide and staring. He is unable to keep eye contact with anyone. He shouts.   'Hey, I've connected with the King.
No you haven't, it's all in your mind.

Yes, I spoke with his vizier, Cassim.

Oh of course you did, hotline to the top was it?

Listen people, I know what we have to do….. Cassim, tell them what you told me……Cassim…..

Silence.

Phil looks at the four people eyeing him. He takes out his mobile phone and stamps on it. He lets out a primal scream.

The Queen recoils in ager. 'That was an unlawful move. You have invoked a third party. Is someone else in your pay?'

The Knave shakes his head. <<No one. I merely played with his mind. He was easy>>

The Queen summons the attention of the group and points in the direction of the Knave. 'See mortals, your earthly desires are an easy target for the Knave. And now he manifests his darkest game plan.'

Phil is throwing his arms around wildly, looking up, looking down. He cannot stop moving. He runs over to Katrin. 'Architect, you possess the knowledge. The discussion we had in the labyrinth, by the loom. I was lazy, I still am. Realize the Queen and follow your heart and your dreams. I must pay Charon, the ferryman.'

And with that Phil turns away from the group and walks away. Katrin follows on and tries to stop him. He resists and gently takes her hand off his shoulder. He continues walking. Katrin stops and tears fill her eyes. The Queen tilts her head slightly as if she felt something but her expression does not change.

Mitch. 'Complete nut, airhead. What was he on?'

Gabriella. 'So, did he like, kill Mendes?'

The Queen. 'No he did not. But he conspired in it. Well you all did.'

Alain tries to get their attention. 'What do you mean he inshpired it. Either he did it or shomeone elshe did it, hic. Why can't any of you hear me?   Hello.'

The Queen. 'I told you. I hear you. But no one else does. Well, tell them Knave.'

<< She speaks a truth, mortals. I desire to take the King and reign supreme. But I did not kill the padre. That was one of yours>>

The Queen. 'You speak a half truth. It was your doing, your move. Perhaps you can shed a light on that Padre?'

Alfonso. 'Surrounded by sinners, caught in the maelstrom of a human virus. Stripped of my dignity and sent here to atone for my sin. He was a vile instrument of the devil!   All liars.'

The Knave speaks. << I have clearly moved the cleric, in an emotional sense, if not a physical one>>

'And he was my piece too! You see how easy the Knave plays you. Summoned to give allegiance to the King, you fall mightily short. Even a holy man, a cleric, a man of spiritual discipline falls prey to the temptation and vice of wrath.' The Queen looks right through Padre Alfonso. 'And the ultimate irony.....you had no technology....you were the most able to resist the calls.....but you failed nevertheless.'

'Why can no one hear me?' Alain finally succumbs to the heady nectar and his body disperses into dust. A fine thread of golden silk trickles down and lands in front of the group.

Katrin. 'What's this got to do with us? It's not like we're Marvel Comic superheroes or anything. I'm just a German architect. And he's a murdering holy man? Jeez, nightmare city.'

<<Well I have to agree, you're small fry. But that's all I need. You'll do. I'm saving the big guns for another time. Because there will be another time. Oh, just out of interest, tell me this, it's baffled me for years, so to speak...... why haven't you lot made 'Casablanca - the Musical?>>

Puzzlement all around. 'Wha?'

The Queen makes her move. 'You were all summoned by the King. To help him. The Jester took charge of that. He got you all here. But the Knave has corrupted you. You are dispensable in his eyes. But I hold the advantage. The Knave can only deal with the physical world. I command the metaphysical.'

Mitch. 'The blogger is gone walkabout. No chef. Dead politician and murderous preacher. I demand to know what your agenda is, Knave. Just me and the ladies? I want some answers.'

<<You want answers?>>

Mitch. 'Unless this is some kangaroo court. I think I'm entitled to them.'

The Knave can see where this is going and a smirk crosses his face. Mitch is oblivious to it.

<<You want answers?>>

'I certainly do. I want the truth!'

<<Tah Dah....You can't handle the truth. Mister, you live in a world that has fallen to chaos. And that chaos has to be tempered. Who's gonna do it? You?*
I have a greater responsibility than you can possibly fathom. You have the luxury of not knowing what I know. You don't like to talk about it, mortals, but you want me, you need me. Whenever you say, 'If I could only turn back time' it's just a punchline for you. For me , it's my destiny. There is no present like the time.
And here's the twist.....I can make it happen, for you. Yes you , peeps>>

The JESTER speaks

And then of course it's what truth does he WANT? The physical truth or the metaphysical truth? It's an important consideration mortals.

The Knave yells back to the Jester. <<They don't want any truth. They want certainty>>

The JESTER speaks

Pfffrrrr....Is anyone going to make a move?

The Queen thinks to herself. 'Well, he's taken the chef and the blogger, useless as they were and the cleric, he's no use to me now either. I need to think. Wrong move, disaster.'

The Knave.   << I sense a retreat. Now my best shot.

Look mortals. It's simple. I'm offering you the once in a lifetime opportunity. To help me turn back the sands of time. To give you order and certainty. You've heard the phrase 'History has an uncanny way of repeating itself', well, shit let's just make that happen. But for the good times. No more chaos, no more tsunami, no more earthquake, no more pandemic. We take the Queen and the King. I take over. Job done.

Make your minds up. Quick. Knight 2 to White Rook 6.

Now, now - here is our move!>>

Mitch pulls hard on the reins of the Knave's steed and takes control. He grabs the Knave's sword and runs up behind the Jester, who is still the channel for the King through Cassim. He thrusts the sword into the Jester's back. Cassim explodes in a cloud of dust and sand. The earth shakes, with all parties falling to the ground, even the Knave.

Mitch. 'You laughed your last laugh! Hahahaha!' He picks up the skull of Cassim and moves his jaw like a hand puppet. 'Let's see who is pulling the strings here, now. You idiots!'

The Knave looks on horrified. <<What have you done - you were supposed to steal his power - not to destroy it!>>

'Who said I've destroyed it?' He mumbles something to the skull of Cassim, and lets it fall to the ground.

'Let me tell you a little bit about debt: It's all of you - those of you, who are on a journey - to become Kings and Queens and adventurers and self-fulfilling spiritual beings.

Deep down, you're selfish pricks. Self centered. And your dreams are built on the back of those who keep the world running.

Those without dreams, daemons and fears. Those who are not troubled and have to sort themselves out on the energy of others. Those who are not damaged. You snowflakes! Those are the men and women of your kingdom you forgot about in your self love, KING! Now rotten corpses like your grand adventure.

From dust to dust. I'll let them sort out what is left. Oh, and by the way Knave and Queen and assorted weirdos, you forgot all about the prime factor in all this while you were advancing your game…the King. Protect the King. That's what I thought this game was all about!! Where is he now?'

He checks his watch, which has stopped.

'Excellent, so the sands of time move on. Now, in the real world, my world, history can and will repeat itself……welcome to the new normal! All I gotta do is turn the sand clock upside down and all is tickety boo. Reset the loop, say every five years…hot dog, my five year plan.

While you were in your own little bubbles I made the game changer. I noticed, unlike you that my watch was still working when we were in some timeless zone. I heard everything. I knew the Knave's plan. It was a good one, but mine is better. And as for the Jester, well he thought he was in charge of the game but he was deluded.

I take the game. I take the sand. I take the silicon. I take the sacred Argan oil. I take everything. And when these commodities are in place, I will remove the virus. But all will have changed. Just a chip off the old block, ha ha. The all seeing Cyclops….

No use for daddy's old tick tock now….' He removes his watch and throws it down.

And as the void opens up a creeping menacing cloud of dust forms. The Businessman is gone.

CHAPTER 16

O! FORTUNA!

The King. 'Cassim, where are you, you foul wretch. Cassim, Cassim, I need some company. Time passes very slowly when your backside can only shuffle on this old stone bench and I no longer have the joy of rattling your chains. Cassim!' Sand blows amidst the walls and weaves around, settling on the ground. All is quiet.

The group wait for the dust to settle in the void. They are speechless at what has happened. The Knave and Queen sit at polar ends, the group in their middle. No-one can quite contemplate what Mitch has just done and said.

Katrin breaks the silence. "Oh god, that's all we need. Another power mad, narcissistic toad calling the shots. At least in the metaphysical world we could get off on a laugh or a dream of something better".

Gabriella. 'We have no way to the King now; The jester guy is dead , as is his skull mate. Hey, was he like actually our driver?'

The Queen shakes her head and sighs. 'I never saw that coming. I expected you, Knave to pull a few crooked moves, but I never imagined how things would turn. We are in a bad place.'

<<Bastard! He must have overheard a conversation to know what he knows. And, fair play he did allude to it. Never saw it coming>>

Gabriella takes a large sigh, straightens up and speaks slowly. 'Right, let's simply put our cards on the table. Why did the the King choose us? Come on, no games. Why?'

The Queen. 'I suspect the choice was inspired by Cassim, old powder skull down there! Though from what has been happening I wouldn't put it past The JESTER having a hand in it.

You all had flaws, as do all mortals, but you had capacity to change and bring about a positive solution. But as for the BUSINESSMAN, he had more than flaws, he had massive ambition.

You may have already worked this out, but you see the King is in control of time. Or was. He has ownership of the great sandclock which determines the passage of time. Him over there, the Knave, has been trying to take the power from the King to shift the sands of time to fulfil his own agenda. He wants some sort of eternal life turntable where time repeats itself. Why, I don't know. He tried to sell you an ethically free never ending future. But by doing that he takes power over me. Oh don't get me wrong. It was tempting at a point. Me, Earth, forever rejuvenating myself and never getting older. But when it came down to it, I could not face a future of constant exploitation on auto-rewind.'

The Knave << I wonder if the King is aware how hard you were fighting his corner, Queen?>>

'I hope he did. I was, but I needed help to get beyond the labyrinth to the 8th rank. We nearly succeeded. The Blogger has given you, Architect, an opportunity to realise yourself and possibly resolve our situation. You see, you are faced with the greatest dilemma.

The businessman wishes to shape the future in order to control it. Did you notice his obsession with his watch. He wants what you wanted Knave. And when history repeats itself, as it will do, for eternity, ethics is no longer necessary. You do what you like in the full knowledge that you can do it again, or you can adapt it, so it's not simply a groundhog day scenario. Now he has control over sand and oil he can manipulate his empire to keep all silicon devices from expiring and put on repeat, forever.

It's groundhog day with benefits. For him certainly.

•

For what it's worth my view on this is that life is a wonderful mystery. Not chaos. Who wants absolute certainty?

Let me check out an example with you. Who wants to know when they will die? No-one. In the midst of an organised clockwork world where intelligence systems ask you to rate your visit without you even requesting it, next day deliveries or your money back, no-one wants an advance warning that they have six months to live.

See? Not always completely logical and not completely foolproof in its design, lady architect. BUT THAT'S LIFE. No power holds the turning of the page. But, I have to concede that as the passage of time moves, so do I get older. Not easy to swallow, is it young model?

Listen, you have to get back to the world of the living and finish this off. Or you live in this madness.'

The Knave. <<Well thank you for nothing for disclosing your version of events. But you haven't told them everything though have you? You haven't told them that the reason you were banished and

incurred the wrath of the, then, virile King, was because you took to the JESTER's bed and conspired with Cassim to topple him from the throne? A knife was it?>>

'I was hardened to my youth. Thought I could hold it all back. Pah, it was my mistake. Oh, and let's get one thing straight. You make it sound like it was some sordid one night stand. Surely you know that the Jester was no mortal ? No. He was a celestial being, a mighty comet. We had an alliance. He would have entered my domain with a mighty crash and changed the world forever. Just as it was 70 million years ago. Yes, mortals, an end to civilisation, AS YOU KNOW IT. How else was I to bring about some change to the order and stop your constant despoiling of my body. Because you were always too intelligent to fall under my earthly viruses, my 'acts of god' as you would call them, always a cure, always an invention.   But….tsss… perhaps a mistake.

And I have lived in the shadows of that mistake, throughout my 4.5 billion years. Enough is enough. So, Knave, we are at stalemate. Why not reveal your motive for this masquerade. You know all about me. They know all about me…. were you just power mad, maybe wanting to boot the King off the throne because you could, jealousy, what? They are usually the prime motives.'

The Knave draws breath. <<Sure, I appear as the Knave, in mortal form. I did it to anger the King because I know he has affiliation with Earth, you. So, what better way to rattle him than mask up as a human being and challenge him. Yep, perhaps a tinge of jealousy. Why choose you above all the other planets?

But that is not my prime drive. If I am not mortal what am I? Like you Oh, Queen, I am a heavenly body….if I may boost my ego…..and I am from a place light years ahead of this solar system. I exist but I am yet to come. On Earth everything seen is in the past, the vast array of stars have already died and it is only the passage of time that keeps them shining. There is life on my planet, but it will not be seen for many millennia. And when that time has come, life on Earth will have expired. With or without a comet. Extinction. No witness.

So I designed a plan to repeat time so that the human can see there is more than life on Earth. That the human IS NOT alone. It'll just take a few more years, well probably a few million actually. So there you are. I had some ambitions but they were not entirely malign. And now the BUSINESSMAN has taken over>>

The Queen is wide eyed with awe. 'I'm lost for words. Really. It's almost romantic!! Despoil my body so that these lot can wallow in some inter-planetary affinity. Tchhh..... if you excuse the pun, I'd rather have a big bang and move on than being on the receiving end of some timeless merry go round.

But the reality is that it has become the perfect storm. The BUSINESSMAN will create a monolithic empire where time is everything. Now you two humans must take up the gauntlet and rid the planet of this tyrant. We owe the King some resolution.'

Katrin speaks. 'What, us? What can we do? We're stuck in this sink hole as of now!'

The Queen. 'Find the loom. Find yourselves. Find his Achilles Heel.'

Gabriella rolls her eyes. 'I guess we're in this for the long haul.'

Katrin. 'Well, as long as it takes.'

The Queen. 'Restore the watch back to time and resolve the chaos.'

CHAPTER 17

THE LOOM

The void remains a dark grey and Phil stuggles to see his way through the assorted paths and warrens. He is perspiring and shaking, aware that he has not eaten or taken a drink for some time, exactly how long, who knows. He stops, checks a position, takes a left, walks fifteen paces and retraces his steps to then take a right.

'For crying out loud, this is like that walk in the souk in Marrakesh. Where the hell is that labyrinth centre and how did I find it so easily originally. I should have taken photos. You complete fool, what were you thinking? But then what's the freaking point, it all looks the same, everywhere. Without a guide I'm buggered. *You still have me.* What, you…. where were you when I needed support back there? You left me drowning big style. *I'm here now.* Oh how very convenient. Abandoned in front of the group, humiliated, questioning my very sanity. And I suppose you're going to guide me to the centre of the labyrinth, eh, don't recall you doing much to help me last time we were here….*oh stop moaning, look follow your instincts, don't try and look for signs, use your imagination, that's what this is all about, you know that…'*

Phil continues to walk ahead, brushing aside cobwebs and dust. He stops. He remembers the first time he witnessed the labyrinth with Katrin. He remembers observing the four pivots from the centre. He remembers seeing the loom. He remembers the bizarre nightmare and the awakening of the knowledge. He remembers his alter ego saying 'keep it to yourself.'

'So, if I had gone your way I would be the only one to try and resolve this nightmare. But I didn't go your way, did I? OK, go fuck yourself, I don't need you to sort my head or soul out.' Phil stops shaking, composes himself and opens his tablet. 'We're here.'

Immediately the void becomes lighter and the way ahead, to the north, south, east and west is clearly visible. And in the centre lies the loom, tangled and worn, wrapped around with threads and thorns, roots and ivy.

He switches on his tablet but there is no signal. 'I don't need this either' he shouts and throws the tablet to the side. He walks towards the loom. What looked like roots and ivy from a distance is in fact fine golden thread. The loom is a simple design and Phil tries to understand how it can be restored to its previous beauty.

He finds the end of a piece of thread and starts to trace it in order to untangle it. He follows the thread and meets several knots where other thread is tangled. He tries to untie the knot. He hears the swirl of wind and a quiet high pitched sigh. He looks around but sees nothing.

He repeats this several times and with each untying of a knot he hears the same sigh.

The envoronment within the centre changes. It is becoming increasingly colder and the general light is being changed by colour. The loom starts to turn, very slowly and the threads start to unwind and grow in length.

'Well done mortal', a voice speaks out. Phil looks behind him. From his position looking out he sees the features of a woman, dressed in a white robe, long flowing hair carrying a distaff upon which is rolled the finest golden thread. A haunting voice sighs out 'See how well the thread is moving now it has no encumbrance'.

'A decent piece of work', another voice, this one somewhat deeper, from the opposite position. He turns and looks to see another female approaching, robed in white and carrying a measuring rod. 'So much easier to measure'.

'You had insight that no other mortal possessed and you were able to pass this on to the Architect'. A voice from the third position rings out. A third female, slightly older than the others, but possessed with grace and beauty, carrying a pair of shears.

'My God, this is insane. Kings and Queens, Knaves and Jesters and now the three Fates. All the hallmarks of some blockbuster movie and I'm standing in the middle of it.   Hold the front page for a minute. Why make me out to be some sort of hero? I left the group without lending a hand. I left the group too lazy to act on my own. And no doubt I'm the focus of their anger at my ineptitude and lack of determination'.

'You gave the architect something she lacked and in so doing allowed her to realise herself. It was there, in her but lying dormant. You showed an act of sacrifice on your part to give her the instruments needed. That was, until the Businessman stole the show. Not your fault, not your design. So, I guess you know our purpose?'

Phil watches the three Fates move in unison until all three surround the loom. The loom comes to a stop. 'As I understand it, you three are, between you the weavers of destiny, inevitability and fortune. I guess you are Clotho, the spinner of thread. It is you who chooses who is to live and who is to die. You, no doubt are Lachesis, you measure the thread with your rod and determine the passage of life. And finally you, fair lady, Atropos, the most feared of you three… the cutter of life. Correct me if I'm wrong but I suspect you had a hand, and a set of shears, in the death of the Politician, am I right?'

'It was his destiny. His lust could not be overcome by any calls for love and empathy. Throughout his journey in the mortal world and the world down here he only had self desire and a desire to exploit others for his own ends'. He's joined all the others who's lives were worthless and is now with the devourer of the dead.'

'And what of me? What length of thread do I have? Am I about to pass through as well?

'Not quite. You have one act to perform and then we will give you the coin you need to meet Charon the ferryman. Without it you cannot pass to the afterlife. So, in order to resolve the chaos that is happening above amidst the Queen and the Knave, and the impending storm that will be committed by the Businessman, you must give the Architect and the Model a sign of our being.'

The three Fates join together and unravel a short length of fine silver thread and pass it to Phil. 'It is his destiny. They must know what we know and pass on the rune to the Businessman in the human world.. The sign must be your act by whatever means you think fit'.   Phil responds. 'I must have a photograph. I'm not going anywhere without one final picture'. Phil picks up his tablet and hurriedly takes a shot of the three. No smile, no pose. And with that the three fates vanish leaving Phil standing and bewildered.

'Find the watch. Use the thread. Adopt the Fates'. These are the three sentences he types into his tablet below the picture he has taken.

A single coin lies on the ground near his feet. It is his commission to the next place.

CHAPTER 18

FINALE

Back in the human world the streets throw up the protest. People demand equality and an end to prejudice. Statues are pulled down and old anthems are challenged. A deadly fever continues to wreak havoc among the rich and the poor. Work grinds to a halt as the economies of the world no longer find the need for conspicuous consumption. People stay at home. A young girl challenges the world and the great powers to wake up and start caring for the one place where life is known to exist, and students challenge the wisdom of the algorithm and succeed in changing entrenched decisions. The planet starts to breathe a little easier and animal life (apart from those in captivity) enjoys a new found, noise free freedom.

And people although worried and frightened at the prospect of their own mortality being taken from them, find time and space for random acts of kindness.

This is not what the BUSINESSMAN wanted.

So, how did it all end readers?

Our two super heroes came out of the sink hole of a desert and made it possible for people to witness the wonder of life and rage against any notion of life repeating itself. The Model campaigned vociferously for an ethic of tolerance while the Architect took on board the push towards sustainable buildings.

Nah, that's not what happened!!

New York City…… Cyclops Towers, now owned and controlled by the Businessman. In his office there are 24 clocks on the wall, each one depicting a different time zone but the times are all the same. Everything is dominated by the tick of the clock.

Mitch's secretary opens the door. 'Sir, there are two ladies in the lobby wishing to see you. They say that you know them from a trip to Morocco.'

He thinks aloud to himself….I thought I'd seen the last of them, what do they want? He speaks to his secretary 'Who are they and whadda they want Martha? Martha, who are they?'

Martha fumbles a little. Mitch is hard to please. She reads from a notepad and tries to get it correct. 'Ummm, Mr Ginsberg, they call themselves Clotho and Lachesis, think I've got that right. They say they have something to give you sir.'

Mitch. 'Show them in and put my next meeting on hold for 15 minutes exactly.'

Enter the MODEL and the ARCHITECT.

Mitch sits at his desk. He does not get up to greet them. He does not suggest they take a seat. 'Hello. Long time no see. Well, let's say long time, my time!! Why are you here and what could you possibly want to give me? And what's with the crazy names?'

Katrin looks at Gabriella. Gabriella looks at Katrin. They both look at Mitch in harmony.

'Shall I start or do you you want to?' Katrin asks Gabriella. 'You start, by all means', replies Gabriella.

Katrin. 'So Mitch, just to bring you up to speed, so to speak. Thanks, but no thanks for leaving us in the void back there in Sahara time. Heard the line from The Pet Shop Boys… Left to our own devices

I probably will…no probably not, you're more a Slim Whitman fan I guess. Anyways, you left us to our own devices. So we went on a little walk…..don't worry, Martha told us you've given us 15, we won't take any longer. Time is money eh? Do you want to continue Gab?'

Gabriella. 'For sure. So we went downside and found the labyrinth. You know it, remember? Well, you don't remember the loom 'cos you never saw it. The loom of fate to be precise. Y'see, amigo the loom was in a bit of a state. All knotted up and such. Well it was until Phil, remember him, the complete airhead, yeah right, until he went back and spent untold hours unpicking the threads and the knots. So when we got there he'd left his tablet by the loom with a single picture on it. It was this.'

Gabriella shows Mitch a picture of the three Fates weaving at a loom. 'Over to you Kat.'

Katrin continues. 'Now those three ladies are called Atropos, Clothos and Lachesis. Phil left a note to say that Atropos had done her work already and the other two could be called upon if needed. And….Hey presto!'

Mitch laughs drily. 'Right, crazy as ever, the weird hippie and naive good time girl. Six minutes left.'

Katrin. 'You left this behind.' She hands over the watch. 'Remember, you said it had stopped, around the time you took out that wacky, weird referee guy. Profound moment, huh?'

Gabriella. 'So as I was saying, we were near the loom and found a fine thread of golden silk, so strong it could have been steel. Then later we found the watch and…..anyways, we got it going . Quite amazing, don't you think? Almost as if it was destined to happen. Tee hee. Seems to keep good time. The thread did wonders for it, though it needed a bit of metaphysical fairy dust but hey, it's tickety boo again. Game changer mebbee?'

Mitch shakes his head in annoyance and disdain. 'Freaking watch. So what? I'll just keep returning, every five years, that's my game plan.'

Katrin looks at Mitch, the clocks above and at Gabriella. 'Three minutes more. But here's the rub Mitch. The thread has your name on it, created by Lachesis. It is she who measures out the thread and determines your fate. The thread is woven into your watch, your life. My, er, colleague here, Clotho has control over your life, and everyone else's for that matter. Seems like your thread isn't that long and oh, yeah....there's a problem with your heart.

You see babe, to achieve what you want you have to mediate the physical and the metaphysical world. We managed to do it for a short time but never for eternity. Just long enough to get your watch sorted. You certainly did not.

Ironic really, but I don't think you're going to be able to engineer your grand plan. Maybe that was why you wanted to turn back time all along. 'Cos of your old ticker. Well, gotta go. Time's up.'

Gabriella and Katrin start to move out but just as they are at the door Gabriella turns. 'Darn it, knew there was something else, umm, could I have a selfie with you Mitch? Me, Katrin and the badass business dictator, might look good in my portfolio... no?, well I guess not. Adios.'

Finale Finale......

Of course, for a while the BUSINESSMAN did make lots of money and usurped power from the elected politicians. He drove his virus laden commodity forward, with the promise of an ethic free future. But he _was_ only human. And this was Earth. The MODEL and the ARCHITECT had found his Achilles heel. And it was time. He was a prisoner of his own foolish beliefs and a hidden genetic disorder. And the ticking watch ticked tocked.

And Pink Floyd had sussed it all out in 1973:

'_And you run and you run to catch up with the sun but it's sinking_
Racing around to come up behind you again
The sun is the same in a relative way, but you're older
Shorter of breath and one day closer to death

Every year is getting shorter, never seem to find the time
Plans that either come to naught or half a page of scribbled lines
Hanging on in quiet desperation is the English way
The time is gone, the song is over, thought I'd something more to say'

A person of no consequence stands on the 87th floor of Cyclops Tower. He has a good view over the Hudson River and all life surrounding. He looks down on the never sleeping streets of Manhattan. People are still protesting, a fever of confusion and emotion continues. He looks up to the sky and he sees a flock of storks flying overhead. He smiles and removes his mask. He flips a coin in the air.

As for the BUSINESSMAN, when the end came, his end, history did not repeat itself. His watch recorded he lived 49 years, 7 months, 7 days and 7 hours….. the magical number 7. And then it stopped.

And at some point in the near future the person of no consequence picks up a copy of the New York Times. He reads aloud from a minor article on page 7 concerned with a sighting of a new comet in deep space. The article describes its size and trajectory . 'It is a very large comet, roughly the size of 20 football fields with a mass of 400 million kilotonnes. NASA has calculated its position, movement and speed and re-assures readers that it will pass Earth at a distance of approximately 34 million miles when it enters our solar system, roughly 150 years away.'

A voice from afar rings out

Well, I think I'll be the judge of that one.

In some place far away, where the sand continues to blow and settle, the King hears a sound. It's the sound of the sandclock being lifted up to its rightful position. The King smiles.

And the MODEL and the ARCHITECT lived a full life, but only the once.

* Taken from the film 'A Few Good Men.'

About the Author

This is Chris's first short novel. It has been adapted from a play of the same title and plot which was written by Chris and a friend from Germany, Matthias, following a trip into the Sahara desert in March 2020, just a few days before most of Europe went into lockdown as a result of the spread of Covid 19. The inspiration for both the play and novel is centred around the many ecological issues facing the planet and the fall of mankind.

Printed in Poland
by Amazon Fulfillment
Poland Sp. z o.o., Wrocław

63998859R00101